BEYOND THE SHADOWS

A CHRISTIAN ROMANCE BOOK 3 IN THE SHADOWS SERIES

JULIETTE DUNCAN

COPYRIGHT

PRAISE FOR "BEYOND THE SHADOWS"

"The end is not a foregone conclusion as Daniel and Lizzy go through the struggles of a rocky marriage and the challenge of alcoholism first without relying on God and then with leaning on Him. It didn't change the circumstances, but their response to past hurts and baggage was vastly different and far more realistic than other Christian fiction on the market." *Snickerfritz*

"This story, for me, was more emotional and really touched down deep in my heart. It was a beautiful story of God's grace, His redemption, His forgiveness and the freedom that is found in all of that." *Heather*

"This series is a definite must read Jesus grace and love is in every chapter, and the power of forgiveness is an awesome thing seen in this book. If you haven't had the pleasure of reading this series you simply must!" *Renee*

"Wonderful story of how the Lord forgives and brings beauty out of hurts, regrets of the life of his children who accept him as their Lord and saviour." *Amazon Reader*

ALSO BY JULIETTE DUNCAN

Contemporary Christian Romance

The Shadows Series

Lingering Shadows

Facing the Shadows

Beyond the Shadows

Secrets and Sacrifice

A Highland Christmas (Nov 2017)

The True Love Series

Tender Love

Tested Love

Tormented Love

Triumphant Love

True Love at Christmas

Promises of Love

Precious Love Series

Forever Cherished

Forever Faithful (coming late 207)

Middle Grade Christian Fiction

The Madeleine Richards Series

CHAPTER 1

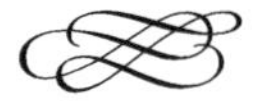

Lakes District UK February 1982

DANIEL THREW the telephone receiver back into its cradle and thumped the wall.

How dare Da return! Twenty years gone, and he waltzes on in, and expects everyone to come running. The hide of the man! Inhaling slowly, he shook his head and fought the anger swelling up inside him. *Not on your life, Da. Not on your life. Even if you're dying.*

Clenching his fists, he stared out the window at the mountains in the distance without seeing them. Just when everything was falling into place. He'd been doing so well. Three months sober. Hadn't even felt like a drink. But now… no, he must stay strong, for Lizzy's sake. He ran his hands through his hair. *God, give me strength. I can't handle this.*

Life had never been so good - he and Lizzy loved living at the College. Why should Caleb expect him to drop everything and come running back to Belfast to see the man he hated most in this world? How did Caleb even get the number?

So many memories. So much pain and hurt. He'd pushed their ugliness away for so long. Why should he be forced to revisit the past? He had a new life. A life full of happiness and peace. Going back was the last thing he wanted to do.

Daniel looked up and clenched his muscles. *That's it. I won't go. Nobody can make me. Not Caleb. Not Da. Not anyone.*

~

"Look Dillon, Daddy's home."

Lizzy held their three month old baby to the window as Daniel drove the tractor towards the shed and excitedly pointed out his daddy. Her heart skipped a beat as she caught sight of Daniel's strong, masculine frame atop the tractor. Wearing his heavy sheepskin jacket and colourful beanie, even from a distance he caused her heart to flutter.

Although almost two months had passed since Daniel began his job as a groundsman at the College in the Lakes District, Lizzy was still in awe of the way God had provided for them. She adored the little cottage where she and Daniel lived. Yes, it was small and basic, but compared to the apartment in Hull, it was paradise. She'd already planned what flowers and vegetables she'd plant when spring came, but until then, she'd busy herself making the cottage into a home.

As much as she loved being a mother and a homemaker, Lizzy missed her friends and her job as a teacher. With Daniel gone early each morning, and the weather too cold to venture outside with baby Dillon, her days were long. Daniel's homecoming was the highlight of each day.

Daniel had surprised her with his devotion to his job and to the Lord. Since giving his heart to the Lord several months earlier while recovering in hospital from his car accident, he'd been hungry for the word and so keen to learn how to live as a Christian. Every day he asked God to give him strength to withstand the hold of alcohol on his life, and every day he gave thanks for one more day of sobriety. He'd also recently made the decision to give up smoking. Lizzy had suggested he wait. It wasn't a problem for her, and besides, staying sober was way more important. But Daniel believed he should. He'd been convicted about how badly he'd abused his body over the years before coming to Christ and was committed to making amends.

Daniel's new found vigour for life warmed Lizzy's heart. The memories of the old Daniel had faded, and rarely, if ever, did she worry about how he'd treat her when he came home from work or whether he'd been drinking. Instead, she yearned for his company more than ever.

He'd taken the responsibility of being the head of his family very seriously, too seriously, Lizzy sometimes thought. Whenever she broached the topic of her going back to work when Dillon was a little older, Daniel stated emphatically there was no need. It was his job to look after her and Dillon. For now, she willingly complied. No use putting undue pressure on their relationship. It was like he needed to prove he could do it.

Lizzy accepted that for now, this was her life. Spring would soon arrive, allowing her to venture out more often. At least they'd gone to town to celebrate their first anniversary just a few days ago. Although Lizzy looked forward to it, leaving Dillon for the first time made Lizzy anxious. She had no qualms about Robyn's ability. After all, being the Principal's wife, and a grandmother of three, Robyn's experience spoke for itself, but Dillon was so tiny, and so dependent. Lizzy knew he'd be fine for the few hours they were out, but it felt strange not to have him with her.

They enjoyed a lovely meal at the Gardens Restaurant in Ambleside, the nearest town to the College. The restaurant adjoined the Lions Head hotel, and Lizzy breathed a sigh of relief when Daniel only briefly glanced at it on their way in. Every time he passed a hotel he was tested, and so far he'd passed with flying colours.

TONIGHT AS DANIEL walked in the door, something was wrong. Normally he'd be happy and his eyes would light up as he reached out for Dillon, but tonight, trouble sat on his face, and Lizzy's heart fell.

She pulled Dillon tighter and followed Daniel to the bedroom. He hadn't even kissed her. Standing in the doorway, she watched with dismay as he pulled off his work clothes and put on a pair of jeans and his favourite rugby jumper without even showering.

She sat beside him on the bed as he pulled on his boots. "Daniel, what's the matter? Talk to me."

"I need to go out, Lizzy. Please don't try to stop me."

Lizzy fought her alarm. It wouldn't pay to over react. This was the exact situation they'd planned for, but hoped would never happen. Before they left Hull, Nessa and Liam explained what could happen as Daniel weaned himself off alcohol, and helped them formulate an action plan. Lizzy found it challenging to step back and allow Daniel to take responsibility for his decisions, and to trust he'd make good ones, especially after all they'd been through. It would've been so much easier for her to take control, but Nessa advised against that.

"You have to give him room, Lizzy. But don't make it easy for him to drink. If he asks you to drive him to town for that purpose, you have to refuse, unless you feel physically threatened. That's a whole different ball game. He's made the commitment to stay sober, but if he does drink, it's not the end of the world. You just go back to square one and start again. Hopefully he'll be strong, and that won't happen."

But it was happening. Why else would he go out on his own? Lizzy breathed in slowly. Her heart pounded in her chest. She held onto Dillon, cradling him into her shoulder. She had to stay strong for his sake.

"Do you want to talk about it?" Lizzy placed her hand gently on Daniel's leg. If only he'd share the reason for this sudden change in behaviour.

Daniel finished tying his laces then stood, pulling Lizzy into his arms.

"I'm sorry Liz. I need to be on my own for a while. It's not you. It's me. I need some space."

It took all her strength not to cry as she gazed into his troubled eyes. If only she had the right words to stop him. Her hands trembled and a sick feeling grew in the pit of her stomach. Somehow she had to retain control of herself. Nessa had said not to plead with Daniel, or to over react. *Easier said than done.*

"Okay. I won't stop you, Daniel, but please don't do anything you'll regret. Just remember, God's with you, and you can draw on His strength to help you get through whatever it is that's troubling you."

"I know that Lizzy. And I'll try." Daniel's normally confident voice strained with emotion. He pulled back from her and sighed dejectedly. "I guess you won't drive me to town?"

Lizzy's shoulders slumped. It was tempting. Maybe he'd change his mind on the way, and he'd come back home with her. But she had to carry out the plan. That's what they'd agreed.

"No, Daniel, I won't drive you. I'm sorry."

"Okay then. I'll walk."

Lizzy bit her lip and blinked back her tears. *God, please give me strength.*

How easy it'd be to give in. She could agree to pick him up at a set time. But that wasn't what they'd agreed. She wasn't to do anything that made it easier for him to drink. Besides, walking might give him time to sort out the problem. *Whatever it was.* But why couldn't he share it with her? Memories of Daniel's deception when he lost his job flashed through her mind. He'd promised never to hide anything from her again. And he'd been such a different person since giving his heart to the Lord. The old Daniel had reappeared, and she didn't like it.

"I'll pray for you." She reached out her hand and gently touched his cheek, her eyes searching deep within his. His eyes flickered. Was he weakening? But then he spun on his heels and headed out the door.

Every bone in her body wanted to follow him, but she remained strong, and instead of racing after him, she cradled Dillon and pleaded to God to keep Daniel safe.

LIZZY'S HANDS shook as she tended to Dillon. Once he'd settled, she picked up the phone and called Paul. As head of the College, Paul provided the counselling to Daniel that was a condition of his rehabilitation program agreed to by the court. Calling him was part of their plan.

"Paul, it's Lizzy here." She gulped as she tightened her grip on the receiver. "I hope you don't mind me calling, but something's happened, and Daniel's walking to town." She bit her lip and forced herself to stay calm.

"I had a feeling that might happen. He got a phone call at lunch time and was in a dark mood all afternoon. Didn't want to talk about it."

Lizzy's mind raced. *A phone call?*

"Did he say who it was from?"

"No, he didn't say a thing. Didn't even finish his lunch."

"That's strange. I have no idea who would have called him. I'm trying to think."

"I tried to talk to him several times during the afternoon, but he just retreated into himself. It's the first time I've seen him like that. I was surprised, because he's normally been quite open."

"So, what do we do, Paul? I'm really concerned about him."

Lizzy held the receiver tightly with both hands. She had to stay calm, but it was so hard.

Paul sighed heavily on the other end of the phone. "Well, first we pray. There's obviously a battle going on inside him. We knew he'd be tested at some stage. We'll leave him alone for a while, and trust he'll work it out for himself. I'll go to town and look for him in a couple of hours. By that stage he might be prepared to talk."

"Thank you, Paul. I don't know what I'd do without you." Lizzy bit her lip, forcing herself to hold it together.

"It's all I can do, Lizzy. We're in this together. Daniel has a good heart, and he loves God. He's just got to learn to trust Him, as we all do. Let me know if he comes home, otherwise I'll leave about eight o'clock. In the meantime, Robyn and I will pray for him, and I encourage you to pray too."

"I will. Believe me, I will."

CHAPTER 2

Daniel, blind to the deepening darkness around him, trudged along the road toward Ambleside. His head hurt, and a weight, heavy as lead, sat in his heart. He should reach out to God. He knew it deep down, but his body craved the release that alcohol would bring. *Just one drink, that's all I need to clear my head. And then I'll think about Da.*

Reaching the outskirts of town half an hour after leaving the cottage, and knowing Lizzy would have called Paul, Daniel sought the least likely place Paul would look. Despite not visiting any of the drinking establishments in town until now, Daniel had kept his ears open. The small tavern on Stockghylle Lane would suit his purposes.

He pulled the hood of his jacket over his head, not only to keep the cold from biting his face, but to avoid being recognised. The tavern could only be reached through the town centre. The few people out scurried about their business, not paying him any attention. He glanced inside the Gardens

Restaurant as he passed by, the memory of his dinner with Lizzy flashing through his mind. *She'll be so angry if I come home drunk. I won't. Just one drink. That's all I need.*

The lights from town slowly faded until he was back in almost complete darkness, with just the occasional lamp glowing from an outside porch providing some indication of where the lane headed. In the distance, the lights from the tavern beckoned. Drawing nearer, Daniel glanced back. No-one was following.

A cold chill ran through his body as he reached the door. The familiar alehouse aroma pulled at him, drawing him in. In the darkened room, Daniel paused to steady his nerves and get a feel for the place. A haze of smoke permeated the stale air, stinging his eyes. Only one room. Several men perched at the bar, and another couple huddled in a corner, deep in conversation.

The stool scraped against the floor as Daniel pulled it out and took a seat. The barmaid approached. His heart thumped. Could he really go through with this? *Am I strong enough to stop at one drink?* He reached for the packet of cigarettes hidden in his jacket pocket and lit up. *Should have thrown them away.*

Instant relief. His heart steadied. Slow, deep breaths. Maybe he could sit on a squash. Let the cigarette do the job. Better than risking getting drunk. *But just one pint...*

"What'll it be, love?" The barmaid stood, hands on hips, her silky voice and voluptuous curves providing a momentary distraction.

Daniel gulped. Was one drink worth jeopardising everything he'd worked for over the past few months? His relationship with God, his relationship with Lizzy, his job? *What am I thinking?*

His hands shook as he drew deeply on his cigarette before grinding it out in the ashtray. Looking up, he held the barmaid's gaze.

"Nothing. Changed my mind."

The bar maid raised her eyebrows. "You sure about that, love?"

Daniel straightened and held her gaze before jumping off the stool. "Yes, I am. Sorry."

Shaking off the eyes staring at him, Daniel opened the door and slipped back into the quietness of the night. He walked a short distance and then stopped, slumping against a light pole. He slid down the pole until he landed on the ground. Relief and anger flooded his body.

What was I thinking? I know better than that. I don't need alcohol.

But something had gripped him deep inside and dragged him towards the abyss. But thanks be to God, he hadn't jumped.

The phone call triggered it. The phone call....

A thousand thoughts swirled in his head. How long since he'd seen Da? He hardly remembered the man who'd deserted Mam and left her to rear him and his seven siblings on her own. He'd assumed Da was dead, but now, to discover he was still alive, and wanting to see him, was too much. Daniel had done his best to put his past behind him and focus on his future with Lizzy and Dillon. But now, here it was, throwing itself in his face.

His eyes drifted closed. Thoughts of God, Lizzy, Da and

Mam tumbled together, over and over. Cold seeped into his body, its invisible fingers penetrating into his very depths. He curled into the foetal position, and remained there, oblivious of the danger he was in, until he awoke to someone shaking him.

Daniel sat with a start. Paul? No, it couldn't be. Not Paul... Daniel's heart fell. How would he explain this to him?

"Hey Danny. Here, put this around you." Paul wrapped a thick woollen blanket around Daniel's shoulders, and remained crouched beside him.

Daniel shivered and pulled the blanket tighter. How long had he been lying there? He glanced up the road towards the tavern. The lights were still on, so not long. He shivered again. He could have frozen to death. How had he been so stupid? But he hadn't given in. A surge of warmth trickled through his body. He fought back his tears and lifted his head.

"Thanks Paul. I'm sorry."

"It's not a problem, Danny, I'm glad I found you." Paul squeezed his shoulder. "Come on, let's get you out of this cold. Have you eaten?"

Daniel shook his head.

"You haven't had a drink either, have you?"

"No, I haven't." Tears welled in his eyes. *But I came so close.*

Paul hugged him. "Well done, Danny. Well done."

Daniel nodded. *Must have been God. Couldn't have done it myself.*

Paul helped him stand and led him to the car.

"Let's get something to eat, Danny."

Paul drove back into town and parked outside Pamela's Pantry. From the outside it appeared no-one was there, but inside, the cafe hummed with background music and hushed conversations.

Daniel inhaled the aroma of freshly cooked pizza. His stomach growled. How long since he'd eaten? Lunch… the phone call had come while he was eating lunch…

"Pizza?" Paul asked as they sat at a table on the far wall, well away from the other late diners.

"That would be great. Thank you."

Paul ordered the pizzas and two coffees and leaned back in his chair.

Under Paul's scrutiny, Daniel lowered his eyes and fidgeted. He had nothing to fear from Paul, but to a degree he'd failed. He hadn't taken a drink, but he'd reacted badly to the phone call, and treated both Paul and Lizzy miserably. *Lizzy.* She must be worried sick. He looked up and sucked in a breath.

"I need to call Lizzy. Is there a phone here?" Daniel's gaze darted around the cafe.

"Don't worry about Lizzy, she's okay. You'll be home soon." Paul's voice was so reassuring.

Daniel relaxed and settled into his chair. The waitress delivered their coffees, steaming and hot, just what he needed. Daniel sipped the sweet liquid greedily, wrapping his hands around the brightly coloured mug.

"So what happened today, Danny?" The deep timbre in Paul's voice should have been soothing, but Daniel gulped and stared at the bright red coffee mug. His heart rate quickened. Time to confess. But could he?

Drawing in a deep breath, he slowly lifted his eyes to meet Paul's.

"I'm not sure." He cleared his throat and took another

breath. "Everything got confused after I got that phone call. It was like something got into me and dragged me along, and I had no control over it. My head was really scrambled, and all I could think about was having a drink."

"Who was the phone call from, Danny?"

Daniel placed his mug on the table and folded his arms, stalling for time. Talking about it would make it real. Was he ready for that? To revisit his past, to rip open old wounds that had haunted him for years. Wounds he'd successfully buried of late?

Maybe it was time to face his past. But did he have to? *God???*

He pushed down the swelling pain deep inside his chest. Yes, he had to.

"It was from my brother. Our Da's come back, and he wants to see me." Daniel narrowed his eyes and pursed his lips. "I don't want to go. I hate the man. Maybe I shouldn't, but I do."

Paul tilted his head and studied Daniel.

"There's a lot of hurt, isn't there, Danny? I can see it in your eyes."

Daniel squirmed in his chair as a wave of anger took hold.

"He deserted our Mam. Left her with eight kids and no money." Daniel held Paul's gaze. "He used to beat her. Us kids'd huddle together in the room next door while he did it to her. The little ones'd cry and want to go to her when they heard her screaming. They didn't know what was going on." Daniel paused, clenching his teeth. "Me and my brother did, though. We hated him for what he did to her. She didn't deserve to be treated like that." Breathing heavily, Daniel's muscles tensed as he fought to control his anger.

"Truth was, we were glad he left, but then we had nothing. Mam did everything to make sure we always had food to eat. She worked the skin off her hands, and it killed her. That's what we reckon. So basically, he's responsible. Maybe not directly, but it was his fault she died." Daniel pulled himself up and leaned forward. "So you see why I'm not that keen to see him?"

Paul drew in a deep breath. "Daniel, I had no idea. I'm sorry." He held Daniel's gaze before continuing. "Something like that goes deep, and I can understand your reaction, especially when it was totally unexpected. No need to make a hasty decision. Take your time to work through it. I'll help you. Whatever it takes."

"Don't have much time to decide. It makes me so angry." He clenched his fists. *Control, Daniel. Control. Breathe...* "He's dying. That's why he wants me to come. How dare he come back just so he can feel better before he dies! What right does he have?" Daniel's chest heaved as he spat the words.

"Danny, calm down. We can work through this together. You don't need to handle it on your own. Okay?"

As Daniel held Paul's gaze, his breathing steadied. Paul really did care. Just like a father should. If only Da had been like Paul, everything would have been different. The tension in Daniel's body eased. He could rely on Paul. That was a good thing. And Paul was offering to help him. *Maybe I should accept.*

Daniel sighed, his shoulders sagging. Time to let go. But his stomach churned. Thinking about Da made him sick to the core.

"Okay. But I'm still not happy about it."

"That's okay, Danny. It's a start. You can grow through this if you're open to God and allow Him to teach you." Paul gave Daniel a warm smile. "He's got great things in store for you, I just know it. He loves you, Danny, and He doesn't expect you to handle this in your own strength."

Tears sprang to Daniel's eyes. Paul had a knack for turning things around.

"There's a verse in 1 Peter you should memorise, Danny. In Chapter 5 verse 7, Peter says to *'Cast all your anxiety on Him because He cares for you'*. And He really does. God cares for you so much, Danny, and He doesn't want you to handle your cares and troubles on your own. You've been learning a lot over the past few months, but this is the first big challenge you've had. Don't let it beat you."

Daniel gulped. No, he wouldn't let Da beat him. Wouldn't give him that satisfaction. *But how do you 'cast all your anxiety onto God?' It's not like you can see Him.*

Leaning back in his chair, Daniel folded his arms.

"Okay. I'll memorise it, but how do you do it?"

Paul let out a small chuckle. "That's a great question, Danny." Paul looked up as the waitress delivered their pizza. "Thank you." He smiled at her and then directed his attention back to Daniel. "Let's give thanks before we eat."

The aroma of the bubbling mozzarella and pepperoni was more than Daniel could bare. His stomach rumbled, but he lowered his head anyway.

"Lord God, thank You for today, and for the challenges that have come our way. Thank You that You're bigger than any challenge we might meet, including this one Daniel's facing right now. Use it to grow him, Lord. Let him open himself to You and allow You to mould and shape him so You can use him to bring glory to Your kingdom. And Lord God, bless this food to our bodies. We are truly grateful for all the good things You give to us, including this pizza. In Your precious Son's name. Amen."

"Amen." Daniel opened his eyes and glanced at the pizza that had been taunting him. "Can we eat now?" He tilted his head and chuckled as he placed a slice on Paul's plate and then one on his own without waiting for an answer.

"Mmm..." Daniel licked his lips as he devoured his first slice in extra quick time. "How good is this?" He flicked the mozzarella that dangled off the edge of his second piece onto its top and took a bite.

Paul nodded his head, his mouth too full to answer.

Paul came back to Daniel's question after he'd eaten his first slice and washed it down with a mouthful of coffee.

"Okay, so how do we 'cast our anxiety on God'?" Paul leaned back and crossed his arms. "Firstly, we need to really know and accept that God is bigger than all our worries and problems put together. Our view and understanding of how big God is determines how much we trust Him. We often limit His ability to work in our lives because our view of Him is too small. The more we learn of God and appreciate His absolute enormity, the more we learn to trust Him. Does that make sense?"

It was a lot to take in, but it did make sense. Daniel inhaled deeply and nodded.

"Good. The second thing is to understand that everyone has difficulties. They come in all different shapes and sizes, but we all have them. Not all the time, and some are more challenging than others, but we all have them. That's life. People often think that problems come their way because of sin in their lives, that it's God's way of punishing them, and they carry guilt and shame that weighs them down, and separates them from God's love and mercy. But that's Satan's trick. God cares for His children. He doesn't punish. He forgives and cleanses, and offers strength and support to get us through any trial that comes our way. If we let Him." Paul smiled at the waitress who came to clear their table. "May we have two more coffees, please?"

The waitress smiled as she wiped the table. "Coming right up."

"But *how* do we let Him?" Daniel asked after the waitress had left. It all sounded good in theory, but how did it play out in reality?

"Well, it's really quite simple when you break it down. Feelings come from thoughts, so even if we can't change how we *feel*, we can change how we *think*. And that's what God wants us to do. Romans 12 verse 2 says, *'Do not conform to the pattern of this world, but be transformed by the renewing of your mind. Then you will be able to test and approve what God's will is—His good, pleasing and perfect will.'* The more we immerse ourselves in God's word, the more our thoughts are transformed, and the less anxiety we have about the troubles we face, because we know God's working in our lives, and that every problem we face is an opportunity for Him to teach us and grow us. So, when it all boils down, it's a decision you make. When problems, worries, and challenges of life come along, you ask Jesus to carry the burden for you. You hand it over to Him. And then you don't take it back. Trust Him to work it out for good in your life, and be prepared to learn and grow as the situation unfolds."

"Okay then." Daniel leaned forward, resting his forearms on the table. "So when I got that phone call from my brother, you're saying I should have just prayed about it and handed it over to God?" He tilted his head and narrowed his eyes. It sounded too simple.

"In a nutshell, yes."

"But my head got all scrambled, and I couldn't think clearly. How was I supposed to do it?"

"It takes practice and commitment, Danny. You're a new Christian, and no-one expects you to react like someone who's been trusting Jesus for many years. The main thing is that you learn from it, so next time something happens, and it will, you'll be more aware, and you can give it to God straight away. But He's not going to judge or condemn you, Danny, and neither will I, or Lizzy, or anyone else for that matter. And you shouldn't beat yourself up either. You didn't take that drink, and that's a huge achievement." Paul leaned closer. "Danny, I really believe God has something great planned for you and Lizzy. I just know it. His hand's on your life, and He's going to lead you into something exciting. I want to encourage you to keep learning and trusting, and keep your heart open to Him. And He'll definitely help you work through this situation with your father."

Daniel gulped. *He's so genuine and sincere. He really does believe what he's saying.*

Paul reached out his hand and gently placed it on Daniel's arm. "Can we pray about it?"

A stirring, deep in his soul, took Daniel by surprise, causing tears to prick his eyes. Never before had anyone offered him so much encouragement. Not Nessa or Riley, or even Lizzy. Paul really believed that God had something special planned for his life. And Daniel wanted it, whatever it was.

"Yes, please." Daniel wiped his eyes and bowed his head, not caring what anyone thought.

"Dear God, thank You for Daniel, and for giving him new life in Jesus. And thank You for being with him right now. We know You'll help him through the days ahead, as he works through the situation with his father. Let him welcome Your thoughts and Your love, and Your forgiving grace and mercy. Help him to cast all his worries onto You, and to allow his mind to be transformed by You so he can see Your good, pleasant and perfect will at work in his life. And Lord, we rejoice that today You gave Daniel the strength to turn down that drink. What a major milestone that is! I ask You to bless him, and Lizzy and little Dillon, and to guide and lead them as they grow closer to You each day. In Jesus' precious name, amen."

Daniel gulped and took a deep breath. "Dear God, everything that Paul said and more. I don't deserve Your love, and I'm sorry for failing You. Please help me do better next time. I want to, I really do." Daniel paused and wiped his tears. "Lord God, You're going to have to work hard if You want me to see Da. You know how I feel about him, but I give it to You, and ask for Your help and guidance. I'm sorry for the way I reacted. Please show me the way. Amen."

"Amen." Paul raised his head and squeezed Daniel's hand. "Danny, you did good. Now, let's get you home to that wife of yours."

~

Lizzy had been praying on and off since her phone call with Paul earlier that evening. Despite her original anguish and the fact that Daniel hadn't returned, she had peace in her heart, and confidence that God was with him.

Well after ten o'clock, tyres crunched on the gravel outside the cottage. Jumping up, she pulled the curtain back and glanced out the window. She let out a small sigh. It was Paul's car, and Daniel was climbing out. She closed her eyes briefly and held her hands to her chest. *Thank You God. Thank You.*

She raced to the door and threw it open. As Daniel walked slowly towards her, Lizzy pushed back the tears that threatened to fall. She held out her arms and threw them around him, pulling him into a tight embrace. His body relaxed in her arms, and as she held him, she closed her eyes and gave thanks once more that he'd come home, whole and sober.

"I'm sorry, Lizzy. I really am. Please forgive me." Daniel spoke softly, as if he was having trouble speaking.

Lizzy lifted her head and searched his eyes. "It doesn't matter, Daniel. Whatever it was, it doesn't matter. You're home, that's the most important thing."

"Yes, it is. Thank you, Lizzy." Daniel pulled her closer, and enclosed in his arms, her heart overflowed with love for him.

"Come inside, Daniel, before we die from the cold." Lizzy took his hand and led him inside into the warmth of the cottage. "Sit down and I'll make some hot chocolate, and then maybe we can talk. Only if you want." As she turned to walk into the kitchen, Daniel pulled her around to face him.

"I love you so much, Lizzy, and I'm sorry for going off like I did."

"Daniel, it's okay. Really." Reaching up, she held his face gently between her hands, and as she kissed him, she made sure he knew he was forgiven.

CHAPTER 3

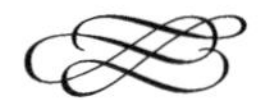

Lizzy and Daniel talked deep into the night. Lizzy's heart ached as Daniel opened up more than he ever had before about his childhood.

"Oh, Daniel. I'm so sorry. Your Da was such a horrible brute." Lizzy's chest heaved. Daniel's story made her sick to the stomach. "Your poor Mam. Why did she stay with him?"

Daniel shook his head. In the dim light, his eyes watered, and Lizzy grabbed his hand.

"I wish she'd left, Liz, but it wasn't the done thing." Daniel inhaled deeply. It tore her apart watching him relive this nightmare. "Women were expected to put up with whatever treatment their husbands dished out back then. Plus, she had nowhere to go, no money of her own, and a handful of bairns to look after. She was tied to him, and that was it." He looked up into Lizzy's eyes. "But we hated him for what he did to her."

"Oh Daniel." His eyes had darkened. The hate was real,

tangible. She didn't blame him - it would be hard not to hate a man like Thomas O'Connor.

"I feel so sorry for her, Daniel. She must have felt trapped." Lizzy gulped. *But wasn't that how I felt when Daniel started hurting me? Trapped, confused, alone.* That gut wrenching pain she'd long forgotten clutched at Lizzy. How terrible to have suffered that pain year after year. *How did his Mam survive?*

"It makes me so angry when I think of all she put up with." Daniel's breath came fast, and his hold on Lizzy's hand tightened.

"But Lizzy," he peered into her eyes, "it hurts me even more when I think of how I treated you. I so hated Da and how he treated Mam, and yet I was going down the same track." He gulped and took a deep breath. "I'm so sorry, Lizzy."

Lizzy reached out and gently wiped the tears rolling down Daniel's cheeks before taking his hand.

"Daniel, I forgave you long ago for all of that. God's changed you. You're a caring, kind man, and I love you with everything I have."

"But I treated you so badly, Liz. I should never have hurt you." More tears welled in his eyes. "I'm so sorry."

"I know, my love. I know you are." Pulling him close, Lizzy rested her head on his. Love for Daniel overflowed from her heart.

Slowly pulling himself away, Daniel wiped his eyes with the back of his hand.

"I could so easily have ended up like him, Lizzy."

"But you didn't, Daniel. You didn't. God's changing you from the inside out, and I know you love me and will never hurt me again. And for that, I am so very thankful." She had not felt quite so much love for Daniel as she did at that moment, and as he kissed her, every nerve in her body tingled as she lost herself in his love.

Nearer to dawn than midnight, sleep finally came, but Dillon had other plans. Lizzy tried to ignore the small cries that would soon escalate to full-blown screams, and snuggled closer to Daniel, pulling the pillow around her ears.

"I'll go." Daniel lifted his head but then dropped it. Lizzy snuggled closer. As Dillon's cries grew louder, she forced herself up. Daniel rolled over. Her head hurt. *If only he'd take a bottle.*

"Come here, little man." Lizzy sighed heavily as she lifted Dillon out of the cradle. His crying stopped and the distraught look on his face changed to a cheeky smile that melted her heart. She pulled him close. "How could I get angry with you?"

Sitting in her chair, with Dillon suckling at her breast, Daniel's heart-wrenching story of his childhood years played through Lizzy's mind. No wonder he'd struggled after getting that phone call. It had been difficult enough for her to forgive her own father who wasn't guilty of any of the atrocities Daniel's father had committed. She couldn't comprehend Daniel's anguish. But God was bigger than all of this, and she knew, beyond a shadow of a doubt, that He'd give Daniel the ability to work through it, just like He had with her.

And He'd already started. Lizzy rejoiced when Daniel told her how close he'd come to ordering a drink, but at the last moment had walked out. Such a major milestone in his rehabilitation, and for that, they'd both given thanks. Of course, more temptations would follow, but for now, this achievement was worthy of celebration. Lizzy decided there and then to surprise Daniel. She'd invite Nessa and Riley and their two children for the weekend, and they'd have a party. The timing was perfect. Daniel turned thirty on Sunday. And maybe, just maybe, Nessa and Riley could help him work through the situation with his father.

Lizzy smiled to herself as she lifted Dillon and gently patted his back. Yes, it would be wonderful to see Nessa and Riley. It may be short notice, but surely they'd come, especially when they knew the reason.

LIZZY'S MIND clicked into gear. No use going back to sleep now. Too early to call Nessa. She made herself a cup of tea and opened her Bible to the book of 2nd Corinthians, Chapter 12.

The words grabbed her as soon as she started reading. *"My grace is sufficient for you, for my power is made perfect in weakness. Therefore I will boast all the more gladly about my weaknesses, so that Christ's power may rest on me. That is why, for Christ's sake, I delight in weaknesses, in insults, in hardships, in persecutions, in difficulties. For when I am weak, then I am strong."*

Just what Daniel needs. He might not like to think he's weak, but if he could grasp the truth of this message, that the God of the universe was offering His strength to help him cope with this situation with his Da, it would be life changing.

Lizzy closed her Bible and folded her arms. *That may be true, but why have You allowed this to happen now, when everything's been going so well?*

Why did You let Daniel's Da come back and upset it all? I don't understand.

I'm really sorry, God but I can't help it. I'm with Daniel on this -

why did You let his Da come back now? If it makes him start drinking again...

Still deep in prayer, arguing with God, Lizzy jumped when the alarm buzzed. *Bother! I meant to turn that off.* She raced into the bedroom. Too late - Daniel was awake and pulling himsclf up.

"I'm so sorry, Daniel. I was going to let you sleep in, but I forgot to turn the alarm off."

"Thanks love, but I need to get up. Too much to do." Daniel stretched his neck and arms, and then stopped abruptly, his face paling.

"Are you alright, Daniel?" Lizzy raced to him and placed a hand on his shoulder, searching his face.

He ran his hands through his hair. His eyes flickered. "I just remembered what happened. It's all come back..."

"Oh Daniel. It's okay." Lizzy wrapped her arms around him. "Maybe you should take the day off? I'm sure Paul won't mind."

Daniel sighed deeply. "No, I need to go. Paul also wants to see me this morning." He lifted his head and looked into Lizzy's eyes. "I'll be alright. Talking about everything last night helped. Thank you, Lizzy." He drew in a long breath and then kissed her gently on her forehead. "I'd better get ready."

As Daniel showered, Lizzy prepared breakfast and tended to Dillon who had also just woken again. She put him in his bouncer and gave him some toys to play with, every now and again bouncing him with her foot.

Lizzy had little idea of what Daniel's job would entail before he started at the College just before Christmas. She soon discovered he was expected to keep everything running, and by everything, they meant everything... from water which tended to freeze in the pipes, to the generators which provided power for the main college building and all the staff accommodation. He was also expected to tend to the cows and chickens the college kept. Lizzy had laughed when he told her that.

Every time Daniel ventured out she prayed for him. Despite being less than half a mile to the main college buildings, at this time of year the road was slippery, and occasionally piled with snow. Although the tractor looked at home as it trundled around the property with Daniel at the wheel, it didn't matter how often he told her it was as safe as houses, she wouldn't relax until he pulled up outside the cottage and turned the tractor off.

The job was perfect for him. He loved tinkering with things, but he also had plenty of contact with people. People who cared about him, especially Paul. Thank God for Paul. He always had time for Daniel. And Daniel always talked about Paul. Almost as if they'd known each other for years, not just a couple of months.

Lizzy smiled at Dillon's chuckles. He was growing so quickly. God had really blessed them with this little man. Her heart swelled with love for him.

"Feel better?" Lizzy smiled at Daniel, her body unexpectedly tingling as he stood there in his work overalls looking spunky. A spark of life had returned to his eyes, much better than yesterday's steely hardness.

"Yes, thank you, love." He bent down and allowed Dillon to grab his finger. "Hello little man. My, how you're growing." Daniel lifted the baby out of the bouncer and sat him in his lap as he ate breakfast.

"You're getting very skilled at that," Lizzy said. "Watch out! He'll steal your toast!"

Daniel chuckled, a warm smile growing on his face. "He's just got a good appetite. Here. Take this, little man."

"He can't eat that yet, Daniel. He's only three months old!"

"He can suck on it if he wants to, surely. It won't hurt him." His eye twinkled with a hint of mischief.

Lizzy shook her head and laughed. "How can I win against the two of you?"

"You don't need to, my love. You have us both eating out of your hand."

"If only..." Lizzy rolled her eyes, but the grin on her face reflected the joy in her heart at having Daniel almost back to normal.

"Here, you'd better take him, and I'll be off." Standing, Daniel drained his mug, then passed Dillon over to Lizzy before placing both his hands on her shoulders and looking deeply into her eyes. "Lizzy, thank you. I mean it. I truly don't deserve you." He leaned forward and pressed his lips against hers. "I love you." He pulled away slowly and held her gaze for a moment before leaving.

Lizzy stood at the window and watched him walk to the shed. Normally he'd be whistling and have a spring to his step, but today he walked in silence with his shoulders slumped. *Must have his Da on his mind. Poor Daniel.* He climbed into the tractor, reversed it out, and then waved before trundling off down the track. Lizzy's heart ached. How she hated to see him struggling like this. They'd been so happy since they'd been here. It wasn't fair.

With the tractor out of sight, Lizzy put Dillon down and picked up the phone to call Nessa. She let it ring longer than normal, but was about to hang up when Nessa finally answered.

"Nessa! Lizzy here."

"Lizzy! Good to hear from you. I hope all's well..."

Lizzy inhaled deeply before relaying the events of the previous day and night.

"Oh Liz, that must have been horrible for Daniel. We always wondered what happened to his father. I guess we assumed we'd never see him again. But now, to turn up like that, poor Daniel. He was such a mean man, Lizzy. No-one held any respect for him whatsoever. It's a wonder I haven't heard from my side about him turning up. But then, I haven't talked to anyone for a while."

"I'm not sure how long he's been back, but Daniel's refusing to see him. Can't say I blame him. He's so upset about it all, but the best thing, Ness, when he went to town last night, he didn't drink! I was so relieved when Paul brought him home, sober."

"Oh Lizzy, that's wonderful! He's making progress then."

"Yes, he is." Lizzy smiled to herself as unexpected warmth flowed through her body. He really was making progress.

She grabbed the receiver with both hands. "Ness, do you think you and Riley and the kids could come and visit over the weekend? It's Daniel's birthday on Sunday, and I thought we could surprise him. I know it's short notice, but what do you think?"

"Sounds great, Liz. I think we can manage it - we don't have much planned, and it won't be a problem to put off Riley's work mate until next weekend. How about we come tomorrow morning? If we leave early, we should get there by about eleven."

"That's perfect, Nessa. You'll stay the night? There's enough room for you all." *Just...*

"Yes, why not? That would be lovely. I've always wanted to see the Lakes District, so I'll look forward to it."

"Great, Ness. We'll see you tomorrow! Safe trip."

WITH THAT SORTED, Lizzy began to plan for their visit. She'd have to squeeze them all into the spare room, but they wouldn't mind. And she'd have to go shopping for extra food, and plan what they'd do. Maybe they could go on a boat ride on the lake. It was still cold, but it'd be fun. If they rugged up well, they'd be okay. The kids would probably like the Aquarium at Lakeside. She'd heard about it, but hadn't been there. And then they could have a birthday dinner for Daniel. Lasagne. Yes, that's what she'd make. His favourite. And a big chocolate birthday cake. She'd better get moving! This was going to be fun. And hopefully Nessa could talk to Daniel about his Da...

~

DANIEL ARRIVED at work and went straight to the workshop. One of the generators had broken down and needed urgent attention. For some unknown reason, the College board wanted to keep the College as self-sufficient as possible, but the old equipment certainly provided a challenge. Not his problem, as long as they kept paying him.

As Daniel worked, the phone call from Caleb played through his mind. He hadn't seen his eldest brother for over ten years, and the unexpected call had scrambled his brain, that was for sure. How close he'd come to taking that drink. Truly amazing he'd baulked at the last minute… or maybe it had been God who'd stopped him? Either way, he hadn't. But having his past dragged up…

But what about Da? Maybe he should go? The churning in his stomach answered his question. But then, talking to Caleb had stirred something deep inside. As the two eldest boys, they'd been the ones who'd stuck together the most against Da, and had helped support Mam. It'd be good to meet up with him and Caitlin again, and meet their two little girls. But what about Da? Daniel thumped the generator. Why wouldn't it do what it was meant to?

Daniel glanced at his watch. Time to meet Paul. Need a break from that monster, anyway. He cleaned up and headed over to the main college building. Paul stood on the walkway outside a lecture room.

"Hey, Paul."

Paul waved as Daniel took the steps two at a time.

"Hey Danny. How are you today?" Paul clapped an arm around Daniel's shoulder and smiled warmly at him.

"Not too bad, considering Lizzy and I stayed up most the night talking."

"Glad to hear that, Danny. All okay, then?"

Daniel shrugged and let out a small sigh.

"Kind of. Still not keen about seeing Da."

"Let's sit down and talk about it. I've got some coffees coming."

Paul's office had a great view of the lake and mountains, but this morning Daniel didn't pay any attention to it. He took a seat on the couch opposite Paul and leaned forward, his body tense.

"I don't understand how he has the gall to come back after all this time. Why couldn't he just leave us alone?"

Daniel fixed his eyes on Paul's and tried to steady his breathing.

"I feel your pain, Danny. But let's talk about it. Maybe your Da wants to make amends before he dies. People often do that. The finality of death puts everything into perspective, and the need to apologise for wrong doings, to sort out relationships that have soured, especially with family, take on an urgency that was never there before."

Daniel gritted his teeth and folded his arms. He shouldn't have come. Da had no right to intrude on his and Lizzy's life. Even if he was dying. Why should he be allowed to feel better about everything when it was him who'd destroyed their lives? No, he really didn't want to hear this. Not even from Paul.

"Sometimes it's selfish. They just want to feel better, to cleanse their consciences. But if the person's genuine, it can be a wonderful experience for everyone. Forgiveness is liberating, Danny. Yes, it's challenging and confronting, but sometimes you only get one chance. Once he's dead, it's too late." Pausing, Paul leaned closer. "Danny, if you don't see him, you might regret it for the rest of your life."

Daniel narrowed his eyes. His chest heaved. How could Paul be talking about forgiveness? He hadn't even decided to see Da, let alone considered forgiving him. And he seriously doubted there'd be any regret.

"No. Can't do it."

"Just think about it, Danny. And pray about it. Forgiveness won't change what happened, but it will change your future. God can begin to heal you deep inside when you're willing to let go of past hurts and forgive those who've wronged you, including your Da. You just need to be open to God and allow Him to do the rest. Will you think about it?"

Daniel sighed heavily. How did Paul always manage to put the guilts on him? He didn't want to hear what Paul was saying, but deep down, Daniel knew it to be the truth.

"I guess so, but to be completely honest, right now, I don't want to."

"I know that Danny. But if you run away from this, you'll miss out on a great opportunity to grow. Growing is never easy. All I'm asking is that you be open to God." Paul looked up as a young girl with long, dark hair walked in with a tray laden with an array of sweet treats and steaming hot coffee.

"Ah, thank you Alicia. Just put it on the table." Paul smiled at her as she lowered the tray and then retreated towards the door. "Coffee smells great, Alicia. Thanks."

The girl smiled in appreciation and closed the door behind her. Paul offered the plate of fancy treats to Daniel. "They know I have a sweet tooth."

"So do I..." Daniel said as he chose a chocolate eclair and took a bite. Cream oozed down his chin.

"These are so good." Paul wiped his face and sipped his coffee before placing the mug on the table. He leaned back in his seat.

"How are you finding it all, Danny? Are you enjoying living here?"

Daniel breathed a sigh of relief. A change of focus was good. His head hurt with all the talk about Da and forgiveness.

Placing his plate on the table, Daniel looked up.

"Yes, it's been great so far. Lizzy's looking forward to the warmer weather so she can get out more, but she loves the cottage."

"She could get involved here. She's always welcome to attend any lectures that interest her, and I'm sure Robyn would only be too happy to look after the baby."

"I'll let her know. She might like that."

Daniel and Paul continued chatting while they finished their coffee. Returning to his generator soon after, Daniel tried to focus on the job, but after a while he got so annoyed with the voices in his head, he threw a spanner on the ground and stomped out.

Standing outside the workshop, he reached inside his jacket pocket and pulled out the packet of cigarettes he still hadn't thrown away and lit one. He inhaled slowly as he gazed through the trees to the lake in the distance. The mountains from the other side of the lake reflected in the water, just like in the post cards at the local newsagent's stands.

As he leaned against the workshop wall, he exhaled slowly, his breath creating little puffs of cloud in the chilly air. He needed this moment - it was so peaceful here. If only his head would settle.

He finished his cigarette and returned to the generator, pushing all thoughts of Da and God out of his mind.

By mid-afternoon, Daniel had the generator re-assembled. He stood back and studied the beast which had tested all his mechanical know-how and pushed his patience to its limit. He had some basic mechanical knowledge, but wasn't formally trained. Only what he'd picked up from some of the jobs he'd had whilst traveling, but it was enough to do the job. Daniel carried the generator to the side of the shed and tried it out on a pump. It worked.

He cleaned himself up, tidied the workshop, checked that everything was in order, and climbed back into the tractor to head home. He stopped to top up the feed for the cows and the chickens, and then trundled back down the track towards the cottage. His stomach rumbled, reminding him he'd skipped lunch. He needed a good feed and a sleep. His body and mind were exhausted.

~

Lizzy looked up as the tractor disappeared into the shed and her heart fell. *Bother!* She'd hoped to have finished cooking before Daniel got home. If only Dillon had behaved… She stood at the stove stirring the sauce for the lasagne. Why wasn't it thickening? No time now either to tidy up. Dirty bowls, saucepans, bags of rubbish… how would she explain it all to Daniel without giving away her secret? At least the soup smelled good.

Finally the sauce bubbled. She gave it one last stir and took the pan off the stove. A few seconds to clean up. She gathered the garbage and threw it in the bin, and stacked the dishes in the sink. Not great, but better.

As Daniel took his boots off on the step, Lizzy patted her hair and pulled her apron off, planting a smile on her face as he opened the door.

"You made it home early, Daniel." She leaned forward and kissed him as he pulled her into his arms.

He peered around her. "So what's all this, Liz? I'm starving..." Pushing her aside, Daniel walked to the stove and lifted the lid on the soup. "What's all this for?" He dipped a spoon in and brought it to his mouth.

Lizzy sighed and folded her arms. "Just never you mind, Daniel O'Connor. There might be a little surprise happening for your birthday, but that's all I'm saying. And don't put the spoon back in! Who brought you up?!" She sucked in a breath. *Why did I say that?* A shadow passed over Daniel's face.

"I'm sorry, Daniel. I shouldn't have said that." Lizzy slid her arms around his waist, leaning her head on his chest. "Did you have that talk with Paul today?"

Daniel sighed heavily. "Yes, I did, but Lizzy, I don't want to talk about it right now. I'm tired and hungry. Can we leave it for now?" He pushed her away and held her at arm's length. "I just want something to eat, and then chill out in front of a movie. Okay?"

"Of course, Daniel. Have some soup now and I'll get some dinner ready shortly." She reached up and kissed him gently. He'd be asleep in front of the television within the half hour. Then she could finish everything in peace.

CHAPTER 4

When Lizzy rose the following morning, the clear sky warmed her heart. The world always looked better with blue sky. While Daniel slept, she'd finished preparing most of the food, including his birthday cake. All she needed do now was decorate it. Dillon also was in a much happier mood. Why wasn't he like that yesterday? The challenge now was to get Daniel out of the house so she could finish the final preparations without him becoming too nosy. Maybe she could ask him to take Dillon for a long walk. It'd probably do them both good. Yes, she'd do that.

To her surprise, Daniel happily agreed. Lizzy rugged Dillon up and sent them off soon after breakfast. She might have an hour or so before they returned. One hour... a lot could be achieved in that time without Dillon to care for. Retrieving the cake from its hiding place in the pantry, Lizzy mixed up the icing and decorated it with Daniel's favourite sweets. That done, she made up the beds in the spare room and gave the bathroom a quick clean. Having guests was exhausting!

The kitchen clock chimed. Lizzy stared at it. Surely it was wrong. How could two hours have gone, just like that? Lizzy's hand flew to her chest. *Daniel and Dillon should have been back. What if something's happened to them?* Lizzy opened the door and peered down the road but they weren't in sight. Maybe they'd bumped into someone - Daniel was always up for a chat. *Breathe, Lizzy. They'll be fine.* Why did she always think the worst?

The kettle was still hot, so Lizzy made a cup of coffee and went outside. Sitting on the steps, she breathed in the clean, crisp air, shivering slightly as a cool breeze brushed her cheeks and neck. The lake would be glistening in the sunshine this morning. Pity the cottage was tucked in a hollow, hiding the lake from view. Never mind. At least she could see the mountains shimmering against the soft blue of the sky. Lizzy inhaled deeply, thankful for such beauty.

A car approached in the distance. Lizzy turned her head. It had to be Riley and Nessa, but where was Daniel? *Surely nothing bad's happened?* As the car came into view, Lizzy stood and waved. Moments later, Riley parked the car in front of the cottage, and he, Nessa and the two children piled out. Lizzy embraced them all warmly.

"Great to see you, Lizzy. And what a lovely cottage!" Nessa pulled back a little to get a better view, and then called out to four year old Jake who was already running around, enjoying his freedom after being cooped up in the car for four hours. "Don't go outside the fenced area, Jake."

Lizzy chuckled. All of this was ahead of her. But where

were Daniel and Dillon? She peered back along the track, trying to cover up her concern, when she saw Daniel running towards them, pushing the pram.

Nessa followed Lizzy's line of sight and reached out her arm.

"I meant to tell you we bumped into Daniel on the way in. No room in the car, so we had to leave him." Nessa laughed as she glanced back over her shoulder.

"Lizzy! Why didn't you tell me we were having company?" Daniel asked when he finally joined them. Panting, he leaned over and rested his hands on his knees to catch his breath. "She's a dark horse, that one." He tilted his head to Lizzy, but his eyes held a twinkle.

They all laughed, and then headed inside with their bags.

Lizzy showed Nessa and Riley to their room, and suggested an early lunch to make the most of the day. They all agreed to her suggestion of a trip on the lake, and so, after a quick lunch of soup and bread, headed off to Ambleside to wait for the ferry.

Lizzy had a quiet word with Nessa while they waited on the wharf. Daniel and Riley stood together with Jake and Cindy playing chasings around them. Nessa cuddled Dillon while she and Lizzy stood a little distance away from the men.

"Daniel seems okay, Lizzy." Nessa turned her head and shot a glance at Daniel.

Lizzy winced, letting out a small sigh.

"On the surface, yes, but it's all bubbling underneath." Lizzy folded her arms and leaned back against the railing, pulling her scarf tighter around her neck to ward off the chilly breeze. "He doesn't want to talk about it at the moment, but it's on his mind. He hasn't said a word since the other night." Lizzy turned to face Nessa. "What he told me about his Da... no wonder he's struggling."

"Daniel's Da was a horrible man, Lizzy." Nessa stepped closer to Lizzy and spoke quietly. "After your call yesterday, I did some checking of my own. It's true he's dying, but Caleb said he's changed, and he wants to put things right with his family before he dies. Riley and I both think Daniel should see him."

Lizzy held Nessa's gaze. "He doesn't want to, Ness. He despises the man." Tears pricked Lizzy's eyes. "I'm kind of with Daniel on this, although I know the right thing is to see him. Maybe you can talk it through with Daniel? He respects you."

Nessa squeezed Lizzy's arm.

"Oh Lizzy. It'll be okay, poppet. You'll see. I don't want to cause any problems, but I'll pray about it, and if it seems right, I'll bring it up, okay?"

"Thanks Nessa. It's so good to have you here." Lizzy's voice caught in her throat.

"And it's good to be here." Nessa patted Lizzy's hand and then glanced at the ferry chugging towards the wharf. "Are you okay, Liz?" Nessa's smile turned tender. Lizzy swallowed the lump in her throat and nodded. Why was it so hard to control her emotions?

Nessa slipped her arm through Lizzy's and walked with her to join the others.

Fares paid, they boarded the old wooden ferry along with a dozen or so other passengers. Riley grabbed Jake's hand to stop him from running around, and Nessa handed Dillon back to

Lizzy before taking Cindy's hand. Daniel followed behind Lizzy with the push chair.

"In or out?" Daniel called from behind.

Lizzy glanced at Daniel over her shoulder. Did he sound annoyed, or was she just imagining it? She pushed the thought aside.

"In? It's a bit cold outside."

Daniel pulled her back.

"Lizzy, did you ask Nessa and Riley to come just to talk me into seeing Da?"

Lizzy's heart sank. Gulping, she raised her head and looked into his darkened eyes. How could she convince him it wasn't one of the reasons when she knew full well it was? It wouldn't pay to lie, in fact, it could make it worse.

Reaching out her hand, she gently touched his arm, but he pulled it away.

"I knew it." Daniel glowered.

"Daniel, I'm sorry. It wasn't the only reason. It was mainly for your birthday."

"I don't want to be hassled, Lizzy. You should have left me to make my own decisions."

Lizzy bit her lip. She'd been caught out.

"I'm really sorry, Daniel. I didn't mean it to be a problem. I was just concerned, that's all, and I thought talking to them might help."

"You need to learn to trust me, Lizzy, and not force things. Let me work through things in my own time."

"I'm sorry, Daniel. I really am." Lizzy reached out again for his arm, and this time he didn't pull away. She searched his eyes, hoping to see some softening. "Will we be okay? I'd hate them to feel unwelcome after driving all this way."

"Yes, it'll be fine." Daniel narrowed his eyes. "But don't push, Lizzy. Okay?"

Lizzy nodded, swallowing hard.

"I really am sorry, Daniel." Lizzy took his hand and walked with him to join the others.

For the rest of the trip, Lizzy clung to Daniel. She had to make things right between them. Why had she thought she could fix everything for him? She still had so much to learn.

The afternoon passed pleasantly enough, although Lizzy struggled to keep her mind focused. She prayed that Riley and Nessa would sense Daniel's reluctance to talk about his Da and not push him. The last thing she wanted was to cause problems between them. She should forewarn them…

The opportunity to speak with Nessa came when they reached the Lakeside Aquarium and the men took charge of the children. Lizzy fell back and joined Nessa. She grabbed Nessa's arm.

"Ness, Daniel's upset."

Nessa faced Lizzy, her head tilted.

"What do you mean?"

"I thought I was doing a good thing." Lizzy's shoulders slumped and she bit her lip.

"Lizzy, what's happened?"

Lizzy took a deep breath and clenched her hands.

"Daniel thinks I asked you here just to talk him into seeing his Da."

"Ouch…" Nessa's eyes widened. "I wondered what you were talking about on the ferry." Nessa slipped her arm around

Lizzy's waist. "Don't worry Liz. We know Daniel, but God's also working in all of this. If Daniel doesn't want to talk at the moment, that's fine. We'll just wait for him to be ready. In the meantime, we'll just enjoy being here with you." Nessa smiled warmly and squeezed Lizzy tightly. How did Nessa always have the right words?

Lizzy pulled herself together and determined to enjoy the outing. She and Daniel hadn't been out much, mainly because of the weather. They strolled through the Aquarium, marvelling at the different types of sea creatures, and laughing at Jake and Cindy's delight at seeing a huge octopus. They ended up at the cafe where the adults enjoyed a Devonshire tea and the children had an ice-cream each. Lizzy stayed close to Daniel and held his hand as often as she could. She wanted him to know how sorry she was for upsetting him, and how much she wanted everything to be right between them. Maybe she was overdoing it, but what else was there to do?

The children fell asleep on the ferry ride back, and by the time they reached the wharf, the sun had disappeared behind the mountains and the chill of early evening began to bite.

"You might have to help me chop some more wood," Daniel said to Riley as they shivered on the way back to their cars.

"No problem, Danny. A good workout will do me good." Riley chuckled as he grabbed Jake and Cindy's hands and led them to the car.

LIZZY HAD ANOTHER SURPRISE, one she hoped Daniel would be happy about. She'd asked Paul and Robyn for dinner as well. She and Nessa quickly bathed and dressed the children, and

Lizzy was doing last minute preparations when Paul and Robyn arrived. Daniel and Riley were still out chopping the extra wood, but came in soon after.

Following the introductions, Lizzy asked Daniel to sort out drinks for everyone. She caught a whiff of cigarette smoke on his breath. It didn't matter. As long as he wasn't drinking. She held his gaze for a moment. Had he forgiven her? She wasn't sure.

Despite the underlying tension that possibly only Lizzy was aware of between her and Daniel, dinner was a joyous occasion. Pleased everyone was getting on well together, she relaxed and enjoyed the friendly banter at the table. Maybe Daniel was just putting on a good show, but he was in good form, as he and Riley competed for the funniest joke. Paul didn't even try to compete, he just joined in with the laughter.

Following dinner, Lizzy brought out the birthday cake and placed it in front of Daniel. His eyes lit up at the assortment of sweets adorning it.

"Happy birthday, my love." Lizzy pressed her lips against Daniel's cheek and squeezed his shoulder. He had to know how sorry she was.

She hoped the sparkle in his eye meant she was forgiven and that everything was fine between them. She'd hated walking on eggshells in the past and certainly didn't want to start again.

Riley began singing 'Happy Birthday' and then everyone joined in. Lizzy beamed at Daniel and clapped her hands as he blew out the candles.

Then Riley pressed him for a speech. Lizzy stiffened and held her breath. *No, not a speech. Please...*

Daniel cleared his throat, shot Lizzy a quick glance she couldn't read, then stood. Lizzy's pulse quickened. She clenched her hands together to prevent them shaking.

~

DANIEL'S GAZE travelled around the table. He didn't deserve such good friends and family. They'd each stood beside him, supporting him when he needed it the most, even when he'd treated them badly. And then there was Lizzy. He'd been way too hard on her. He hadn't meant to react the way he had - she was only trying to help. And he loved her so much. Daniel swallowed hard. What would he do without her?

He inhaled deeply and lowered his eyes, his fingers resting on the table. He owed it to each of them to be honest, but could he really share what was on his heart? Bare all? How could he do that? Maybe he should just thank them for coming and leave it at that. It'd be the easiest way out, but no, it wasn't enough. He closed his eyes and took a deep breath. *God, I really need your help...*

His mind calmed as Lizzy took his hand and squeezed it gently. *Yes, he could do this.* He needed to. For Lizzy.

Daniel lifted his gaze and smiled warmly at Lizzy. He cleared his throat again.

"Thank you all for coming, especially Nessa and Riley for coming so far, and for Lizzy for organising this without me knowing." He paused for a moment and swallowed hard. "I haven't been the best lately, and I'm sorry for my bad behaviour. I haven't been handling things too well since I got that phone call. It was the first big challenge I've had since becoming a Christian, and I blew it."

Paul started to interrupt, but Daniel held up his hand.

"Let me speak. I owe everything to God and to you people. You've all been so patient, and have shown love when I haven't deserved it. Being forced to think about my childhood and Da stirred up old emotions that have been eating away at me. I know you all believe I should see him, and forgive him, but it's not that easy when all I see when I think of him is a despicable man who beat my Mam." Daniel breathed slowly as he clenched his fists. *Control yourself, Daniel. Don't lose it in front of everybody.*

He steadied himself. He had to do this. "Each of you have had something to say, and God's been pricking me, even though I've been trying to ignore Him. But it's eating away at me, and I can't ignore Him forever, I know that, so despite how I feel," Daniel paused and gulped, "I've decided to go."

Daniel held Lizzy's gaze, her tears causing a lump to appear in his throat. She squeezed his hand.

"I have no idea how God can change the hate I have for Da into anything else, but I'm willing to give it a go and trust Him. You'll all need to pray hard, because He's going to have a difficult job."

Lizzy stood, and in front of everyone, wrapped her arms around him and kissed him.

"Daniel, we're all behind you." He squeezed back the tears that threatened to fall. He didn't deserve this much love. Breathing deeply, he hugged her back.

"Daniel, can we pray for you?" Paul asked as he stood and placed his hand on Daniel's shoulder.

Unable to utter a word, Daniel nodded.

"Lord God, thank You for working in Daniel's life. Such a special and much loved man, and one whom I'm convinced You have Your hand on. Bless his decision to trust You, and I ask that You change his hate for his Da to love and forgiveness. Do a wonderful work in his heart, Lord God, and use this to bring him closer to Yourself. Guide and lead him in the days ahead. Thank you Lord God. In Jesus' name, Amen."

"Amen."

Daniel inhaled deeply as a wonderful sense of calm flowed through his body. Why had he struggled so hard against God? He had so much to learn about living as a Christian.

THE FOLLOWING MORNING, Paul was the guest speaker at the church in Ambleside, and Daniel looked forward to hearing him preach. Making the decision to see Da had changed everything. Like a light switch being flicked on in his head, all the negative thoughts he'd been harbouring had been replaced with positive ones, and he felt much happier.

Daniel and Lizzy took their seats in the small stone church, with Riley and Nessa alongside. The children had gone to Sunday School, so only Dillon was left to care for, and so far he was behaving.

Daniel took Lizzy's hand. He'd never believed church could be so enjoyable. In the past, he'd gone just to keep Lizzy happy, but now he went because he wanted to. And now he was back on speaking terms with God, Daniel sensed the presence of the Lord and it warmed his heart.

Paul stood to begin his sermon. *God, please speak to me this morning. I need to hear from You.* Although it was the right decision to see Da, Daniel had no idea how to handle it. If it was up to him, he'd probably end up punching Da, but that definitely wouldn't go down well in anyone's eyes, let alone God's.

Paul began by reading from Mathew 5, verses 43 - 47, *"You have heard that it was said, 'Love your neighbor and hate your enemy.' But I tell you, love your enemies and pray for those who persecute you, that you may be children of your Father in heaven. He causes his sun to rise on the evil and the good, and sends rain on the righteous and the unrighteous. If you love those who love you, what reward will you get? Are not even the tax collectors doing that? And if you greet only your own people, what are you doing more than others? Do not even pagans do that? Be perfect, therefore, as your heavenly Father is perfect."*

As Paul spoke about God's undiscriminating love to all people, Daniel listened intently. God wanted him to show the same undiscriminating love not only to those who were easy to love, but to those he didn't like, or even hated, i.e. Da. *Can I do that? God, I'm sorry, but I'm not ready for this...*

Paul continued; "Jesus instructs us to live by a higher standard than what the world expects, a standard that's impossible to attain through our own efforts. A standard that can only be achieved through the power of God's Holy Spirit working in our lives.

"What's impossible for man, becomes possible for all those who give their lives to Jesus Christ through the power of the Holy Spirit living in their hearts.

"And there's more... God not only expects us to love those we find hard to love, He also wants us to pray for them. In my experience, I've found it's infinitely easier to love someone I dislike when I've prayed for them, because when we pray, God's able to open our hearts to seeing people the way He sees them, instead of the way we naturally see them.

"Loving your enemies, and praying for those who grieve you leads you into release, freedom and happiness..."

Maybe that's what I can do. Pray for Da. Even if I don't feel like it. God'll have to do the rest, because I can't.

Daniel squeezed Lizzy's hand. This would be the hardest thing he'd done in his life.

AFTER CHURCH ENDED, they had lunch in town before Riley and Nessa headed back home. As they were leaving, Riley took Daniel aside and handed him an envelope, telling him not to open it until they'd gone.

Daniel gave Riley a puzzled look.

"What's this?"

"Just wait until you open it."

Daniel obeyed and put the envelope into his top pocket.

Driving back to the cottage after waving Riley and Nessa off, Daniel reached into his pocket and took out the envelope. His eyes popped. Two hundred pounds! This was too much. Opening the note, he read it aloud.

"Daniel and Lizzy, we want you to put this toward your trip to Ireland so that all three of you can go. Please accept it as a gift that doesn't need repaying. We give it to you in love, and pray that God will work His way in your lives as you obey Him. All our love, Riley and Nessa."

Daniel's eyes blurred with tears. "Liz, pull over." A sudden breathlessness took hold, along with a fluttering in his chest, as if a small bird were inside trying to escape. He couldn't believe it. No-one had ever been this generous to him. What had he done to deserve this?

Lizzy pulled over and wrapped her arms around him.

"Daniel, are you okay?" Lizzy's voice was gentle and concerned as she whispered in his ear and stroked his hair.

Daniel nodded and slowly controlled himself.

"I just can't believe it, Liz. I'm in shock."

Lizzy laughed softly. "I think it's God's way of telling you you made the right decision."

Daniel let out a huge breath. He still couldn't believe it. *Two hundred pounds!* It would have taken him months to save that much.

He took Lizzy's hands. "Seems like God really wants us to go, so I guess we'd better book our tickets."

Lizzy beamed a smile at Daniel and threw her arms around his neck before planting a huge kiss on his lips.

CHAPTER 5

Lizzy rose earlier than normal the day they left for Belfast. With so much still to do, her mind had been active all night and she had trouble sleeping. After Daniel had made the decision to go, everything happened quickly, leaving little time to organise it all. Boat from Liverpool was the easiest and cheapest way to get there, but it meant an early start to arrive in time for the 10.30am sailing. Dillon had to pick that day to be difficult, and it didn't help that Daniel still couldn't drive. The year without his license was dragging.

"Come on, Daniel, we have to leave. Turn it off." *How does he have time to watch television?* Lizzy huffed as she did a last sweep around the kitchen and lounge. "Dillon's ready. His pram's in the car. The bags are all at the door."

"Okay, love. Calm down. We've got plenty of time."

She stopped and glared at him. "No, we haven't. What if we get lost?"

"We won't. Trust me."

Lizzy rolled her eyes. That was the problem. Every time Daniel navigated, they took twice as long to get anywhere. But she daren't say that.

She bent down and picked up Dillon, his little face still red from crying. She needed to calm down for his sake. "Come on, little man. Please be good." Patting his back, Lizzy carried him to the car and placed him in the baby seat. She sighed with relief as the front door closed and Daniel appeared with the bags.

Sliding in beside her, Daniel extended his hand and placed it on her leg. "Sorry Liz. I haven't been much help."

Lizzy gave an exasperated sigh. "It's okay, Daniel. I know you're nervous."

"I guess we've got everything?"

"Yes, Daniel, we've got everything."

Lizzy pulled out the choke and sent up a quick prayer of thanks when the car started first go.

"Just as well we don't have the Escort anymore, hey love?"

She threw him a wry look as she thrust the gear stick into first and sped off down the track. *Yes, but I miss my old car...*

Once on the open road, Lizzy gave the Fiesta a good workout. Daniel turned the radio up and leaned back in his seat, humming to the music. Dillon thankfully had fallen asleep soon after leaving.

She shouldn't have been so short with Daniel. He was nervous about meeting up with his family, especially his Da. She knew that. Despite all the discussion they'd had, and all the praying they'd done, he was still nervous. Who wouldn't be? She should be grateful he hadn't turned to drink as he would have in the past. Yes, she should've been more patient and understanding. Lizzy sighed as she sped past a slow lorry. *God, will I ever get it right?*

Lost in her thoughts, and with Daniel and Dillon both fast asleep, the miles slipped away. Everything was fine, and they made good time until they hit a foggy patch. Lizzy slammed on the brakes as the cars ahead came to a standstill. Daniel jolted forward and almost hit his head on the dash.

He straightened himself and faced Lizzy. "Whoa, love. You trying to kill us?"

"No Daniel. But look at this!" Lizzy raised her hand and waved it around. "If it doesn't start moving, we won't get there in time."

"Calm down, love. You can't do anything about it."

"I know, but what if we miss the boat?"

Daniel peered out the window. "Where are we?"

"About half an hour out. Can you check the map? I think we turn off soon. That's if we ever get moving again." Lizzy gritted her teeth and tapped the steering wheel.

Daniel opened the map and studied it as the traffic began to slowly move again.

"Have you found where we are?" Lizzy glanced at him. "I think I can make out a sign up ahead."

"Not sure, love. Still looking."

"The lorry's covering the sign. I need to make a decision. Left or right?"

"Give me a minute..."

"We haven't got a minute, Daniel!" Lizzy's pulse quickened. Why couldn't he read a map? How he'd managed to get himself around the world was beyond her. Too late to get across, no choice - she had to go right. She sighed heavily. *God, I hope this is the right way...*

She breathed easier when a sign for the port showed up ahead.

"See, nothing to worry about." Daniel's grin was infectious and she couldn't help letting out a small laugh as she shook her head.

"Yes, but we're still cutting it fine."

"Maybe, but we'll be right, Liz. You'll see."

"Ten minutes until check-in closes. We'll have to run when we get there."

Reaching the car park, Lizzy frantically searched for a spot. Finally finding one, she pulled in and brought the car to an abrupt halt.

Grabbing a trolley, Daniel placed their bags on it as Lizzy picked up Dillon and almost threw him into his push chair. He needed a feed, but he'd have to wait. The ferry wouldn't.

People milled about, the din hurting her ears. So many counters. So many people. She scanned the area frantically.

"Over there, Liz." Daniel pointed to the check-in counter to his right, and steered the trolley towards it.

"I never want to do that again, Daniel. Two minutes more and we would've missed it."

"But we made it, love, that's all that matters." Daniel winked, dispelling her angst in an instant. It worked on her every time.

"Yes, we did. Just. I've got to feed and change Dillon before we board, but I can't see anywhere to sit. Can you find somewhere, Daniel?" Lizzy lifted Dillon out of his pram and gagged. "Poor little man. No wonder you've been upset." She wanted to comfort him, but held him at arm's length.

"I'll take him to the bathroom to change him. I won't be long." Lizzy reached up and kissed Daniel on the cheek. "I'm sorry for losing my patience, Daniel."

Daniel smiled and brushed her cheek with his fingertips. "It was both our faults, Lizzy. I'm sorry too."

Lizzy smiled as she walked to the bathroom. She hated being angry with Daniel.

She found the bathroom easily. The whole area needed a clean, but at least it had a changing bench. Laying Dillon on his back, she tried to placate him as she battled to clean him.

"Come on little man. Work with me. The sooner you do, the sooner you can be fed."

With Dillon finally cleaned and smelling much better, Lizzy hurried back to Daniel, now standing alone with the bags.

"Boarding's begun, Liz. Here, let me take him."

Lizzy handed Dillon over and followed Daniel to the end of the slow moving queue.

"Where do we go, Daniel?" Lizzy called once aboard the ship. She didn't like the way she was being jostled. Everyone seemed to be in a hurry.

"Follow me," Daniel called out over his shoulder.

She followed him to a quiet area with sofas on the left side of the ship.

"We can stay here all day if we want. I'll put our luggage in one of the lockers."

Lizzy sat on one of the sofas, thankful Daniel knew his way about, and began to feed Dillon.

As the ship pulled out of port, Lizzy realised she had no

idea whether she'd get sea-sick or not, never having been on the open sea before.

She soon discovered she wasn't a good sailor. Not long out of port the ship began to roll and a wave of nausea hit her. Her body instantly felt clammy. She threw Dillon into Daniel's arms and sprinted for the bathroom, just making it.

She wasn't the only one who spent most of their time in the bathrooms heaving up green bile.

Morning sickness has nothing on this. Maybe I won't make it to Ireland after all.

~

WHILE LIZZY SPENT most of her time either in the bathroom or laying prostrate on the sofa, Daniel walked up and down the boat with Dillon, often in his arms, and occasionally in the push chair. Every time he passed one of the bars, his taste buds played havoc on his brain, and he had to tear his gaze away from the kegs holding the amber liquid.

If it hadn't been for Dillon, it would've been so easy to give in. *Maybe Lizzy being sick is God's way of keeping me sober.* Daniel grinned at God's sense of humour. He'd have to tell Lizzy when she was well enough to understand. She might not appreciate it after being so sick, but oh well. Tell her anyway.

The first few hours passed slowly. Dillon didn't want to sleep. Daniel had hoped the movement of the boat might've settled him, but it had the opposite effect, and Dillon had also been sick once or twice. By mid-afternoon, Daniel was at his wits' end. Lizzy was in no fit state to help -she could hardly even feed the baby, let alone do anything else. After Dillon had been fed, Daniel decided to try again, and put Dillon in the push chair and walked him briskly up and down the deck. Not daring to stop, Daniel guessed that Dillon might have finally fallen asleep after five or so minutes. He continued walking for another few minutes and then slowed down enough to take a look. Yes, the wee little man had finally given in. Hallelujah!

Daniel retraced his steps and lay down on the sofa opposite Lizzy, half lying, half sitting, one leg on the sofa, the other slowly rocking the push chair. He'd just rest his eyes for a few moments while Dillon slept...

Although his body rested, his mind was active, and strange images flitted through, jolting him into semi-awareness every now and then. A picture of Mam sitting at the dinner table peeling vegetables flashed through his mind. Mam...

DA HAD BEEN SENT home from work again that day. Every day he went, hoping to get a day's work, but more often than not, he and many others were sent packing without any work or pay. On those days, Da would spend his time out back, drinking with Micheal O'Leary from next door. And on those days, Mam would more than likely suffer at Da's hands.

Summer in the Cregagh Estate offered many opportunities for two eight year old boys to fill their time. Daniel and his best mate from next door, Colin O'Leary, spent most of their summer holidays fishing down at the River Lagan, or tramping along the river's edge and canal paths, stopping now and then to throw in a line. They'd set off in the morning, and wouldn't return until late afternoon, usually with at least a couple of good sized trout to give to their Mam's, who depended on the boy's efforts to help feed their families.

That day started like any other…

"Daniel, now don't you go getting yourself into any mischief, you hear?" Mam handed him a brown paper bag containing two large oat cookies. Mary O'Connor was so short, that at eight years of age, Daniel almost stood eye to eye with her. He couldn't help but notice how big her belly was getting. He sighed. Another bairn on the way. Another mouth to share their food with.

"No Mam, we'll be good. Promise."

"Off with you then. And make sure you bring home a good catch today." Daniel chuckled at his mother's words. Exactly the same as every other day's.

"We'll try, Mam." He flashed her a cheeky grin and darted quickly out of her reach. Mam had an annoying habit of ruffling his hair, but she did it because she loved him, not to annoy him. He didn't mind, really, but it was still better to escape it if he could.

Daniel ran out the door, leaving the chaos of his home behind him, and jumped over the piles of assorted objects lying discarded in the backyard and into the yard next door to meet up with Colin.

"Hey Colin, you ready?" Daniel called out through the back window where he knew Colin would be. He daren't go inside. Colin's Mam was worse than his own. Her humongous body smelt, and she had long hairs coming out from under her arms. Despite that, she was quite a nice person - from a distance.

"Coming," Colin replied.

A moment later, the short red headed boy with freckles

appeared on the door step. He too held a brown paper bag in his hand.

"What have you got today?" Daniel asked.

"Strawberries and cream."

"Go on with you, Colin O'Leary. Let me look."

"No. It's all mine."

"You've got oatcakes, the same as me."

"No I haven't."

"Yes you have."

"Doesn't hurt to pretend."

"S'pose."

The two boys continued their friendly banter as they headed off towards the river for their day of fishing and exploring.

"Hope we don't see those crazy Catholics today," Colin said as they took their spot on the bank of the river. In the distance, army helicopters hovered over the city as they did every day, but the boys ignored them.

"If we do, we'll shoot them with our sticks." Daniel held up the long stick he used for fishing and pretended it was a gun, shooting the hated Catholic kids they sometimes had the ill fortune of meeting.

"Yeah, we'll get 'em good." Colin joined in, and before long, they'd killed all the Catholics that dared to walk along their path.

Later, sitting on the edge of the bank with their legs dangling close to the muddy water, they munched on an oat cookie each, pretending they were strawberries and cream.

"Do you even know what strawberries taste like?" Daniel asked Colin.

"Yeh. Like a Gobstopper."

"No they don't. I had one once. It was all soft and sweet and tasted like heaven."

"What does heaven taste like?"

Daniel thought for a moment. "Like a Gobstopper." He peeled over backwards in laughter, and Colin joined him.

Sitting up suddenly, Daniel looked at Colin. "We'd better catch some fish. I'll get a backhander if I go home empty handed."

"Yeah, me too."

For the next hour or so, the boys concentrated on fishing, and between them caught five good sized trout.

"Guess it's fish for dinner again." Colin's shoulders slumped beneath the weight of his bucket. "Don't like fish."

"Better than broth."

"Guess so."

The boys trudged back to their homes. They would've stayed out longer, but if they did, they'd expect a hiding from their Da's for being late and for getting up to no good. Not that their Da's ever asked what they actually did. Their Da's just assumed the boys always got up to mischief.

At their front gates, the boys separated. From the front, the brown brick terraced houses looked exactly the same. Two storeys high, and stretching as far as you could see, the row of houses was cold and lifeless. Daniel hated the brown brick, and wished he could paint it a bright colour, but he'd never be allowed.

He paused before entering the house to listen for Da. The coast was clear. He tiptoed in and placed the fish on the kitchen sink. So far so good. He snuck out of the kitchen and had his first foot on the threadbare step when a heavy hand landed on his shoulder. He froze. *Not again, please, no.*

He turned around slowly and looked into Da's bloodshot eyes.

A SHRIEK ROUSED Daniel from his sleep. He sprang up, dazed. Where was he? Shaking his head, he looked at the source of the noise. Dillon was awake and screaming, his little arms thrashing in the air. Lizzy wasn't about.

Standing, Daniel undid the clip on the push chair and lifted the screaming baby to his shoulder.

"There, there, little one. Da's sorry."

Daniel froze. Where had that word come from? He never, ever used it for himself. He'd been dreaming about his childhood. And Da... A sickness developed in the pit of his stomach. Tomorrow he'd be seeing him again - face to face.

Daniel sat back down and held Dillon close to his chest, gently patting him on his back. Maybe it'd been a bad idea to come back. Could he really face that man again after all he'd done? How many beatings had he and his brothers and sisters suffered at the hands of that cruel man? And how many times had Mam been so battered she could hardly get out of bed? And now he'd come back, wanting to make amends. *Twenty years too late, Thomas O'Connor. Twenty years too late.*

"God, you're going to have to give me the strength to do this. I can't do it on my own. There's just no way."

Daniel sighed deeply. "There there, Dillon. It's okay." He looked up as Lizzy came towards him, still a little green, but better than before.

"How are you feeling, my sweet?" Daniel pushed thoughts of Da away for the moment and gave Lizzy his full attention.

Sitting beside him, she reached for Dillon. "I've had better days. I never knew anyone could be so sick. And the boat's even stopped rolling." Shaking her head, she smiled weakly at Dillon.

"What's all this nonsense, then, my little man?" Dillon calmed down as soon as he was in her lap. Amazing.

"We're almost there, love. Should be docking within the half hour." Daniel placed his arm gently around her shoulder and pulled her close. "I don't know if I can do this."

Lizzy pulled away slightly and held his gaze. "No, you can't, Daniel, but God can. He's brought you this far, He'll be with you the rest of the way."

He gazed into her eyes, so strong, and so right. God was here, and wouldn't let him down.

~

As THE SHIP sailed towards the dock, darkness settled over Belfast, the lingering colours of twilight slowly giving way to the artificial lights of the big city.

Lizzy stayed close to Daniel as they lined up with all the other passengers jostling for position to get off first. She felt claustrophobic with so many people so close.

"I need to get off," she whispered to Daniel. Slapping her hand over her mouth, she attempted to calm her nausea.

"Are you going to be sick?" Daniel's voice was gentle and full of concern.

She nodded, and then pushed her way through the crowd

to get to the side of the boat, immediately feeling better as she gulped in the fresh air. She turned her head slightly as Daniel laid his hand on her shoulder.

"Are you alright, love?"

She smiled weakly. "Yes. I just couldn't handle being in that crush. Let them go. There's no hurry, is there?"

Daniel shook his head. "No, not really. We can stay here until it clears." He paused, placing his arm around her shoulder. "Lizzy, do you mind if I have a smoke?"

Lizzy slipped her arm around his waist and held his gaze. "You're nervous, aren't you?"

"Yeah, you could say that."

"Go on, then. Have a cigarette if it'll help."

"Thanks love." Daniel pulled the packet from his jacket pocket and lit up. "I will give up, Lizzy, I promise."

When he planted a kiss on her head, she leaned in to him. It didn't matter. She loved him just the way he was.

CHAPTER 6

"I feel bad we've made them wait," Lizzy said as she and Daniel walked along the corridor towards the Arrivals Hall at the end of the long line of passengers.

"Don't, Lizzy. It's only a few minutes between first and last off."

"They might think we're not coming."

"It's okay, Lizzy. Stop panicking."

"I'm not panicking." Lizzy shot Daniel an angry glance and straightened her shoulders defensively.

"Yes, you are."

But her grip on the push chair tightened the closer they got. What would his family be like? Would they have anything in common? As much as she tried, her English accent was impossible to hide. What would they think of her? Would they see her as someone who considered herself better than they, just because of her accent, even though that's not what she thought? Was she over-thinking it? They were just people, after all. And God was with her. She should never forget that. As long as she remained open to Him, His love and kindness would shine through her. She inhaled deeply. *God, please help me get along with them. Let your love shine through me, I pray.* Her heart pounded, nevertheless.

And there they were - standing together in a group holding a 'Welcome, Daniel & Lizzy' placard in the air. Lizzy hung back slightly to the side of Daniel, allowing him to take the lead. She squeezed his arm as he paused and shot her a quick glance. Their eyes met for a brief second. *Yes, they could do this.*

CASTING his eyes over the small group standing before him, some faces familiar, others, not so, Daniel's gaze settled on a tall, lanky man, not much older than himself wearing a pair of black high-tops, acid washed jeans, white T-shirt and denim jacket. The man's neck, adorned with a tattoo of a cross, suggested his body could well be a work of art under his clothes. His dark hair, shaved on the sides, was spiked on top. Daniel recognised him immediately.

"Caleb!" Daniel strode to his brother and wrapped him in a bear hug before holding him at arm's distance. "You haven't changed a bit, man, apart from maybe this." Daniel tilted his head to get a better look at the tattoo.

"Yeah, that's new. Grand to see you, Danny. It's been too long." Caleb grabbed Daniel's hand and shook it vigorously, his dark eyes lighting up.

"Yes, it has. Way too long."

The tall young woman on Caleb's right caught Daniel's attention. *No, it can't be... or can it?* "Grace?"

The young woman's dark smoky eyes were familiar. Yes, it was Grace. His little sister had morphed into a classy beauty. Slightly over-dressed in dark designer jeans, knee-length boots and fitted red jacket, she could have just come off the cat walk. Her immaculate make-up accentuated her naturally good looks, and was topped off with heavily permed dark brown hair.

Grace nodded as her eyes watered. Daniel held her tight, squeezing back his own tears. How long had it been? She must have been twelve when he'd gone to live with Nessa's family, and Grace and their next sister down, Brianna, had been sent to live with Aunt Hilda in Londonderry. He hadn't seen either of them since.

He pulled away and held her at arm's length. Her tears had escaped, and black streaks spiralled down her cheeks. Pulling a clean handkerchief from his pocket, Daniel gently wiped her face.

"Grace, I don't believe it. Look at you! You're all grown up. I wouldn't have recognised you on the street."

"You've changed a bit too, Danny, you know." Her eyes sparkled as a cheeky grin grew on her face. Taking the handkerchief from him, Grace continued dabbing her eyes, and once composed, turned to Lizzy and held out her hand. "And you must be Lizzy. Welcome." She smiled broadly at Lizzy, continuing to exude such confidence Daniel was amazed. Grace had always been outspoken, but he'd never expected this.

Lizzy returned Grace's smile and took her hand. "Thank you, Grace. It's lovely to meet you."

Daniel cringed at the look on Caleb's face. He'd almost forgotten how Lizzy sounded, but here with his siblings, her well-bred English accent was blatantly obvious. He placed his arm gently around her shoulders.

"Lizzy, this is Caleb, my brother, and Caitlin, his wife." He directed Lizzy's focus to the young woman to Caleb's left. She'd changed in the years since he'd last seen her too, which in fact had been at their wedding, not long before he'd packed up and left. Although she'd put on weight, Caitlin's round jolly face would cheer anyone.

Lizzy smiled at them both and said hello before her gaze dropped to the two young girls standing between them.

"And this is Imogen and Tara." Caitlin lowered her eyes to the twin girls and gently pushed them forward. "Say hello to your Uncle Danny and Aunt Lizzy, girls." Dark eyes gazed up, but the girls clung to Caitlin's legs and wouldn't budge.

"It doesn't matter," Lizzy said to Caitlin before stooping to the girls' level. "You have very pretty hair ribbons. And I love your sparkly shoes."

The girls looked down at their shoes before inching closer to their mother.

Caitlin shook her head and rolled her eyes. "One day they'll learn to be social."

Lizzy let out a small laugh as she stood. "They're very cute. I wouldn't worry about them."

Dillon let out a huge cry. Daniel bent down and picked him up from the push chair. "And this is our little man. Dillon Patrick O'Connor. He obviously didn't want to be left out!"

Everyone laughed, and then Caleb finished introducing the other family members. He apologized for not being able to gather all the siblings together, but said he'd fill them in on the others later. At first glance, Daniel would never have recognised the two youngest girls, Aislin and Alana, who'd only been six and seven when the family had been torn apart. On second glance, he gasped. Maybe it was their eyes, or the shape of their faces, he wasn't sure, but their resemblance to Mam unnerved him. The two girls held back and clung to their partners. Had they only come out of curiosity? Probably. It'd be up to him to make a move - standing there like a stunned mullet wouldn't achieve anything. He leaned forward and kissed them, trying to avoid thoughts of Mam before shaking hands with their partners.

"Hey Danny, we thought we'd stop at Molly's Tavern on the way home to get a bite to eat. You up for that?" Caleb asked as the group moved slowly towards the exit.

"Sounds good." Daniel looked to Lizzy and raised his eyebrows. "Liz?"

Lizzy nodded as she took Dillon from him. "I'll need to feed this little man soon, but he can wait a little longer." She glanced around quickly. "Nowhere to feed him here anyway. So, yes, that would be nice."

"Great. Grace has room for you in her car. Let's go." Caleb picked up one of the little girls who'd been pulling on his leg as he tried to walk. "What's up Immi? Can't you walk today?"

The little girl shook her head and put her thumb in her mouth, her large round eyes fixed on Lizzy and Dillon as she peered at them from the safety of her father's shoulder.

~

LIZZY SHOT Daniel an amused look as they approached Grace's car. Why wasn't she surprised to see a hotted up red sports car?

"Don't worry... Caleb will take your luggage." Grace laughed, her grin widening into a full, easy smile that lit up her face.

"Phew! I did wonder how we were all going to fit," Lizzy said, warming to Grace's unexpected sense of fun.

Caleb, Caitlin and the girls had been tagging along behind, and stopped in front of a less trendy but more practical Ford Escort parked beside the sports car. Lizzy reached for her cross. Twice in one day, memories of the not too distant past had surfaced, bringing with them a sense of nostalgia.

Caleb grabbed the luggage and squeezed it into the boot.

"We'll see you there," Grace called out and waved as the sports car sprang to life and surged forward. In the back, Lizzy held on tight. Grace drove fast, but had complete control. She obviously loved driving. Or was she trying to impress?

"You've done alright for yourself, Grace." Daniel shot her a sideways look as he caressed the leather seats.

Lizzy studied the two of them. They must have been close when they were young, there was an ease between them you wouldn't expect after so many years apart.

"You could say that. I decided to make something of myself, so I went to University." Grace shifted down a gear as the lights changed, and the car gurgled to a stop. She turned her head and gave him a playful look. "Your little sister's a lawyer."

Daniel's eyes popped and he let out a low whistle. "Wow. You've certainly done more than alright. So, is there a Mr Grace anywhere?" Daniel's eyebrows lifted and he wore a cheeky grin.

Lizzy winced and glowered at him. *Don't ask questions like that, Daniel!*

Grace straightened her shoulders defensively and lifted her chin to a haughty angle. The playfulness disappeared from her face.

"No. Not interested in men." Her voice was crisp and measured.

An uncomfortable silence took over for several seconds. Lizzy bit her lip as she watched from behind. *Come on Daniel, be sensitive.*

"Sorry, Grace. I didn't mean to upset you." He sounded apologetic. But would Grace let him off that easily?

Grace looked him up and down. Lizzy held her breath.

"Apology accepted."

Lizzy exhaled slowly and her body relaxed. *Thank goodness for that.*

Moments later, Grace made a hard left before screeching to a stop in the Tavern's car park. "Looks like we're the first ones here."

"I'm not surprised." Daniel's grin held warmth and affection.

"What do you mean, Daniel? Don't you like my driving?" Grace threw out the challenge.

"I didn't mean that. Your driving's grand, Grace. Just teasing." Daniel chuckled and shook his head.

Lizzy, relieved the tension had diffused, smiled to herself

before handing Dillon over to Daniel so she could squeeze her way out of the back. This was going to be a good week.

The others arrived within minutes, and they all wandered into the Tavern together. Lizzy walked beside Grace and tried to strike up a conversation. She'd like to get to know her. Lizzy couldn't quite put her finger on it, but despite Grace's outward confidence, Lizzy was convinced she was hiding something.

The group stopped in front of the menu board. Main meals were still being served, but had they been any later, only the snacks' menu would have been available. A table, large enough to accommodate the whole group, was available, but Lizzy excused herself before taking her seat and took Dillon into a quieter, more private corner to feed him.

From her vantage point, Lizzy studied the group. Each of them had a story, beginning in their family home all those years ago.

Caleb and Caitlin appeared happy enough, and so did Grace, on the outside. And the two girls who'd hardly said a word? What was going on there? There were still three more. Brianna, and the twin boys, Shawn and Brendan. And then there'd been Dillon, who'd only lived a matter of hours, and who they'd named their own little man after.

Daniel appeared with a menu in his hand, interrupting her thoughts.

"How's the little man doing?" Daniel lowered his gaze to Dillon, moving the cover Lizzy had placed over him slightly so the baby's face was visible.

"Almost done. Another few minutes should do it." But Dillon stopped sucking as he caught sight of Daniel, his big round eyes lighting up. He kicked his legs and pulled his mouth away, letting out a huge chuckle.

"Well, that's it. No more for you." Lizzy propped him up and patted him gently on the back. "You can go to your daddy in a minute."

"Let me order first, Liz. I'm just getting a burger and chips. Here's the menu."

"Just get me something light, Daniel. I don't feel like much after being sick all day. Maybe a plain sandwich?"

"Okay love." He stood and squeezed her shoulder. "Are you alright?"

Lizzy sighed deeply and nodded. "Yes, kind of. It's been a long day."

"I know. My mind's spinning." He glanced at the group seated behind him and leaned closer to her. "I don't really know any of them."

"I gathered that." Lizzy looked up at him, searching his eyes. "Do you think we've been sent here for a reason, Daniel?"

"I was wondering that. Seems Grace has something going on, that's for sure."

Lizzy put Dillon back in his push chair and straightened her top.

"Yes, I agree. The more I've thought about it, the more I believe God's brought us here, Daniel. It might be an interesting week."

Daniel nodded as he pulled his finger away from Dillon's grip.

"Yes, I agree. I hope I'm up to it."

"You will be, Daniel. God's with you, don't forget."

"Just as well He is. I wouldn't be here without Him." Daniel gently ruffled Dillon's head, causing the baby to gurgle and kick. "I need to place our orders." He gave Lizzy a peck on the cheek before turning and walking away.

"Don't be long. Dillon wants you," Lizzy called after him.

Daniel turned his head and grinned. "I'll be as quick as I can."

~

DANIEL ORDERED the meals and returned to the table, picking Dillon up from the push chair and placing him on his lap. He picked up his squash and took a sip. If only it was a Guiness. Was he really strong enough to do this? He sighed resolutely. He had to be. For Lizzy and for Dillon. For himself. *God, please give me strength.* He took Lizzy's hand. Her squeeze assured him he wasn't in this alone. *Thank you God.*

The conversation around the table was mainly directed at them. Daniel's siblings knew very little about where he'd been since he'd left Ireland over ten years before, nor how he and Lizzy had met, nor what he was doing now. He answered their questions as best he could, deferring to Lizzy at times, and asked them what they'd been doing too, since he knew less about them than they knew about him.

Caleb had married Caitlin just before Daniel had left and still worked at the shipyards where their Da had worked until he lost his job. They still lived in the Cregagh Estate, not far from the house they'd all lived in as kids. Grace had returned to Belfast to study, and now lived in an apartment in the city on her own, near to where she worked. The two girls, Aislin and Alana, lived together in a flat with their boyfriends, Joel and Conall, and were shop assistants. Joel was a carpenter, and Conall a painter. They all seemed to get on well together, but it soon became apparent they saw little of the family. It was only at Caleb's insistence they'd come.

"We don't know where Brianna is," Caleb said. "She took off with some dude a while back and hasn't been in touch since. We're worried about her, aren't we, Grace?"

Grace nodded. "We tried to find her, but I don't think she wants to be found." Her face paled. "She didn't get on too well with Aunt Hilda, and ended up mixing with a bad crowd." Tears welled in her eyes. "I'm sorry." She took the handkerchief Daniel had given her earlier out of her pocket and dabbed at them.

"Don't apologise, Grace," Lizzy said, squeezing her hand. "You obviously care about her."

Grace nodded and sniffed. "Yes, very much. I hope she'll come back one day."

"I'm sure she will. We'll pray for her."

A faint smile appeared on Grace's face but disappeared quickly.

"And Shawn and Brendan - that's another story." Caleb took a sip of his drink. "Shawn took off overseas with his girl a year ago - last we heard, they were in America. Brendan - well, he's a no hoper. Drinks way too much, and he's in and out of trouble all the time. He's in the clink at the moment for assault." Caleb shook his head and shrugged. "Not much we can do for him. Not that we haven't tried, hey Grace?"

"Yes, we've tried just about everything, but he doesn't want any help." Grace sighed heavily.

"Well, I know what that's like," Daniel said. "If there's one thing I've learned, it's that you can't make people do something they don't want to do. I hate to say this, but it might take something bad to make him wake up to himself."

"Did something bad happen to you, Danny?" Grace asked, touching his arm lightly.

Daniel hesitated. How much should he say? They would all have known about his own stint in jail after he'd assaulted Liam, Nessa's brother, but they knew very little about his journey since then. How could he sum everything up in a sentence?

"Well, yes, it did. I almost killed myself in an accident a few months back, didn't I Liz?"

Lizzy nodded as she linked her arm through his.

"Almost losing everything made me come to my senses, and I haven't had a drink since."

"I wondered why you were drinking squash and not the Black Stuff," Caleb said.

Daniel paused for a moment, shifting in his seat as all eyes turned on him.

"Yep. I can't afford to drink." His gaze quickly travelled around the group. "It's not easy. I'd love to have a drink, but that's the way it is." He drew in a deep breath. "But I'm okay with it now."

"Good on you, Danny," Caleb said. "I'm glad everything's worked out for you. I've had a few problems myself, haven't I, Caity, and I've cut back." He put his arm around his wife and gave her a kiss on the cheek. "But we're good now. I had to behave once these two came along." He tilted his head towards the two little girls sitting on his other side, colouring in quietly.

"Seems like our Da left his mark on a lot of us," Daniel said as the meals began to arrive.

While they were eating, Daniel continued his conversation with Caleb.

"I got really down about five years back and hit the grog hard. Almost lost my job, and I hate to say it, I almost lost Caity too, but she stuck by me and helped me get myself together. We go to church every week now, and I've only had the occasional slip up since."

"Stop the lights! You serious?"

"Yeah man. We're regular church-goers. Does that surprise you?"

"Not really. It's just that Lizzy helped me find God too." Daniel shook his head and chuckled. "Who would'a thought..."

"Yeah, my mates were all gobsmacked, I tell you. They still give me a hard time, but I don't care. My life's much better now."

"I'd have to agree with you. I'm only a few months down the track, but I couldn't imagine life without God anymore."

The buzz around the table lowered. The others were listening, but Grace leaned back with folded arms and narrowed eyes. *Something's definitely going on with her.*

Daniel squeezed Lizzy's hand and caught her eyes for a second. Yes, it really did seem that God had brought them here this week.

A short while later, once the table had been cleared, Caleb stretched his neck and yawned. "You both must be tired. I know I am. Call it a night?"

"Yes, it's been a long day," Daniel replied.

"Let's get you home, then." Caleb reached over and picked

up one of the girls. Following his lead, everyone else stood and began to stroll out to the cars. Before they all went their separate ways, they all agreed to catch up again in the next day or so, even the two girls who'd hardly said a word.

Grace dropped Daniel and Lizzy at Caleb and Caitlin's home and promised to see them again the following night after work. As Daniel climbed out of the car, Grace hugged him tightly and planted a kiss on his cheek.

"It's been good to see you again, Danny. I'm sorry I got short with you." Her eyes twinkled, but he couldn't read what lurked behind her well-groomed facade, which he was now sure it was. Daniel smiled warmly and hugged her back.

Grace then turned to Lizzy and held out her hand. "It's been lovely meeting you, Lizzy. I'll look forward to seeing you again tomorrow."

Lizzy took Grace's hand and smiled affectionately. "I'll look forward to it, too, Grace." She then leaned in and gave Grace a hug.

Daniel placed his arm around Lizzy's shoulder and waved to Grace as she sped off. Waiting for Caleb and Caitlin to climb out of their car, a wave of nostalgia swept through Daniel. It was all so familiar. Under the dim street lamps, the brown brick was as cold and unwelcoming as ever, although the small garden out front did help to soften it.

They followed Caleb and Caitlin inside. The layout was exactly the same as the house he'd grown up in, but the modern furnishings and light clean colours gave it a totally different feel. Daniel breathed a little easier.

Caitlin led them upstairs to the spare room. Decorated in warm yellow, a double bed dominated the space, along with an old chest of drawers standing on the wall at the foot of the bed. A cot for Dillon was tucked in beside the bed.

"I hope you'll have enough room," Caitlin said as she pulled the blind down and closed the yellow polka dot curtains. "I know it's a bit tight."

"I'm sure we'll be fine," Lizzy said. "It looks very homely. I just hope this little man doesn't wake everyone up in the night." Lizzy smiled at Dillon and grabbed his hand and gave it a waggle.

"Oh, don't you worry about that. We're used to it with our wee ones. They still wake up sometimes." Caitlin chuckled as she fussed with the bed covers.

"Leave that, Caitlin. We can sort it," Lizzy said, giving Caitlin a warm smile as she bounced Dillon in her arms.

Caitlin stopped fussing and squeezed her way back towards the door. "I'll go downstairs and put the kettle on, but if you'd like to freshen up first, the bathroom's through here." She pointed to the door beside the bedroom at the end of the hallway.

"A shower and a cup of tea before bed sounds great, doesn't it, Daniel?"

"Yes. Grand idea. It's been a long day," Daniel replied with a yawn.

Caitlin chuckled. "I'll leave you to it. Come down when you're ready."

After Caitlin had disappeared down the stairs, Lizzy took out their night things and suggested Daniel have first shower while she changed Dillon.

When she looked up, Daniel was peering out the window.

"Are you okay, Daniel?"

"Yes, it's just strange being back. Come and have a look, Liz." He pulled her gently to his front and slid his arms around her waist. "See that house over there? The one with the street light out front?"

Lizzy followed the direction he was indicating and nodded.

"That's our old house."

As Daniel stood with his arms around Lizzy, gazing across the roof tops, the years fell away, and for a moment he was transported back to a far less happier time. He sighed deeply.

"Are you alright, Daniel?" Lizzy leaned back and tilted her head towards him so their eyes met.

He spun her around gently and traced his fingertips along her hairline. "Yes Lizzy. As long as you're with me, I'm more than alright. I couldn't imagine being here on my own."

"Oh Daniel." Lizzy searched his eyes as she lifted her free hand and gently caressed his face. "I can't imagine how you're feeling. But God's with you too, and He'll be there to help."

"And for that, I'm forever grateful." He lowered his head towards hers, and just as their lips met, Dillon let out a cry.

Daniel pulled away and poked Dillon's little chest. "You, little man, have great timing..." He shook his head and chuckled. "I guess we can pick up where we left off later." He flashed Lizzy a grin full of promise, and picked up his clothes before walking to the shower.

CHAPTER 7

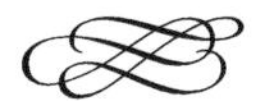

Daniel tossed and turned. Sleep eluded him. Dillon let out the occasional whimper and Lizzy breathed steadily beside him. Throwing off the covers, Daniel slid out of bed and put on the dressing gown Caleb had lent him before tiptoeing out the door and into the hallway. The floorboards creaked on the steps even though he purposefully only trod on the edges. A wonder the noise didn't wake anyone.

Outside, the cold night air took his breath away. He pulled the dressing gown tighter and lifted the collar around his neck. If only he'd put on a heavier coat. Too late now. Walking briskly, Daniel reached the end of the street and turned left. The streets were silent, but in the distance a dog let out an occasional bark and a car horn blasted.

Reaching Teldarg Street, Daniel's heart raced. So many memories. *This is stupid. Shouldn't have come.* He gulped and fought to remain calm. What had Paul said? *'Doing the hard thing is the way to grow...' Okay, God, I'm willing, I think, help me grow...*

As he walked slowly along the street, memories of the day Mam died floated through his mind. Mam'd been sick for a while, but none of the kids really knew she was dying. She kept saying God would heal her. But He didn't. None of the kids could understand what had happened when they were separated. Daniel looked up. *God, why didn't You heal her? I know You could have.* Daniel wiped the tears pricking his eyes.

He stopped in front of the house. Very little had changed. Ugly brown brick. A shiver ran down his spine. Such a cold house. No-one ever wanted to leave the only fire and venture upstairs to their cold beds. No, the house held few happy memories. If only Da hadn't drunk so much, things might've been different. Daniel closed his eyes and inhaled slowly, trying to control the tension growing in his body.

Clenching his hands, he looked up. His whole body quivered. *"God, how do You expect me to face Da? You know I've been praying for him, but right now, I despise the man. I'm sorry, but that's how I feel."* Daniel took a deep breath. *"I'll be honest - I don't want to be here, God. I know I'm fighting against You at the moment, so You're going to have to help me. Okay?"*

Daniel took one more look at the house before turning and slowly retracing his steps. Could he face the man who'd destroyed their family?

When he slipped back into bed a short while later, Lizzy stirred and wrapped her arms around him. He closed his eyes and finally, sleep came.

"WELL DANNY, YOU READY?" Caleb asked as the four adults sat at the table finishing breakfast.

Daniel tensed. *I'll never be ready.* He breathed deeply as his heart pounded in his chest. Was it too late to pull out?

Lizzy took his hand and squeezed it. *No, this is stupid. I've got to do it. Get a grip, man.*

He looked into Caleb's eyes. "Don't think I'll ever be ready, but I'll go anyway. We'd better leave before I change my mind."

"Why don't we pray before you leave?" Caitlin asked, looking at Daniel, her round face warm, jolly and caring.

Lizzy squeezed Daniel's hand again and smiled at Caitlin. "That would be wonderful."

"Let's pray then."

Daniel bowed his head with the others. Caitlin began, praying for God to be with Daniel as he met with his father. Caleb continued, and thanked God for bringing Daniel back to them, and asked that he might find it within himself to forgive Da.

Daniel hesitated. He should pray, but a lump had formed in his throat. His heart beat faster, and then Lizzy began to pray. He breathed out a slow breath. *God, thank you that Lizzy knows exactly how I'm feeling.*

"Lord God, we ask that You meet Daniel exactly where he is, and that You expect no more of him than he's capable of right at this moment. Reward his willingness to be obedient, even if he's struggling with it. Let him draw on Your strength, Lord God, and may he know Your peace and love deep in his heart."

Daniel squeezed back tears. He needed God's touch more than ever. What was expected of him was more than he could do on his own. And to be honest, he didn't understand why he should forgive Da. The man didn't deserve anything from him. *God, You really need to work this out in my life. I'm sorry, but I can't say something I don't mean. You'll have to perform a miracle.*

THOMAS O'CONNOR WAS in a Rehab place run by the Salvation Army. As Caleb parked the car, Daniel steeled himself. Too many things in his head - his time in the building next door intruded into his mind.

"Not sure if I can do this, Caleb." Daniel sat, frozen in his seat.

He closed his eyes and breathed slowly. He'd let everyone down, God included. Why couldn't he just trust God like Paul had encouraged him to do? Why was it so hard?

Maybe Lizzy should have come. She gave him strength. *No. I need to do this on my own.*

Daniel turned his head and studied Caleb. He would never have expected his brother to be so solid.

"How did you manage it, Caleb? I'm really struggling with going in there." Daniel reached into his jacket pocket and took out a cigarette. "Mind if I smoke?"

"Go ahead."

Daniel offered the packet to Caleb, but he refused. Daniel lit up and inhaled slowly.

"I felt much the same as you, Danny. When Da first made contact a few months ago, I straight out refused to see him. He kept ringing. Every night. I refused to speak to him." Caleb shifted in his seat. "Caity spoke to him though. Asked her not to, but she ignored me. She finally convinced me to see him."

Daniel leaned his arm on the window sill and tapped the ash onto the ground.

"What d'you do when you saw him?"

Caleb drew in a long breath and chuckled quietly.

"You might not believe this, but I cried."

"Go on. You cried?"

"Yep. Balled like a babby." Caleb's eyes twinkled.

Daniel shook his head. "That's the last thing I'll be doing."

Caleb leaned forward and looked Daniel in the eye.

"You might be surprised, Danny. He's not the git you remember. There's hardly anything left of him, and he really does seem sorry for what he did. Says he's found God." Caleb winced and took a breath. "Don't know whether he has or not, but me'n Caity, we decided to believe him. You decide what to do, but we figure he doesn't have much time left, and it's better to let it all go. Grace doesn't feel the same. She won't have anything to do with him."

Daniel took another drag on his cigarette and then folded his arms. "Guess we'd better go in. Get it over with. You might need to hold me back though."

"You'll be okay, Danny. I think you'll be surprised."

"We'll see."

WHILE THE TWO little girls entertained Dillon, Lizzy helped with the breakfast dishes.

"Daniel seemed very nervous," Caitlin said, hands deep in suds.

"Yes, I'm concerned about him. He's been struggling with

the whole thing ever since Caleb called." Lizzy stopped wiping and stared out the window. *God, please be with Daniel... he must be there by now...*

"I'm sure he'll be fine, but would you like to pray again?" Caitlin stopped washing and faced Lizzy.

"That would be great, Caitlin." Lizzy smiled warmly at Caitlin. Such a wonderful surprise to discover they shared a common faith.

Caitlin dried her hands and then sat at the table. Lizzy took the seat opposite, and with their hands joined and heads bowed, they prayed for Daniel and his father.

"God's with him, Lizzy." Caitlin's eyes sparkled as she raised her head.

Lizzy nodded, pushing back the tears that had welled in the corners of her eyes. "Yes, I know He is."

Caitlin squeezed Lizzy's hand, and then turned her attention to the little girls standing before her.

~

WALKING along the corridors of Calder House, a cold, nauseating lump sat heavily in the pit of Daniel's stomach. Every step brought him closer to Da. He recalled the verse Paul had asked him to memorise ... *'cast all your anxiety onto Him because He cares for you...'*

'Okay God, I'm casting my anxiety onto You now. You've got me this far, which is a miracle, but I don't know how much further I can go.'

Daniel glanced inside each of the rooms he passed. The beds were full of men. Thin, sickly men, older than he, but any one could've been him in the years ahead. But God had saved him from this. How close to the edge he'd come, but God had stopped him tipping over, and given him new life full of hope and purpose.

And now he had the opportunity to reunite with Da. Was it possible Da was truly sorry for what he'd done? Daniel needed to be open to that possibility. To give Da the benefit of the doubt, like Caleb had done. But could he really do that?

'God, I'm really not ready for this...'

The closer Daniel got, the harder his heart pounded. Caleb stopped in front of the last door on the left.

"This is it, Danny. You okay?"

Daniel inhaled deeply and shook his head. He couldn't do it. How had Caleb made himself walk through that door the first time? Must be made of stronger stuff.

"Give me a few minutes..." Daniel walked to the end of the corridor and leaned against the door frame. Shivers ran up and down his spine and his hands shook. Why had he agreed to come? What would Lizzy think if he didn't go in? To come all this way and baulk at the last moment?

Daniel turned as Caleb placed a hand on his shoulder.

"Take your time, buddy. There's no hurry."

Daniel looked up and nodded. If anyone understood how he was feeling, it was Caleb. He took some deep breaths and gritted his teeth. He had to do this.

Lifting his chin, Daniel forced himself to speak words he didn't want to say.

"I don't want to see him, Caleb, but I'll do it. Once. That's all."

Caleb squeezed Daniel's shoulder and held him at arm's length.

"That's all that's expected of you, Danny. No more, no less."

Daniel followed Caleb into the darkened room. Six beds in total, three on each wall. Five occupied. Daniel scanned each bed. His eyes rested on the last bed on the right. It had been almost twenty years, but he would've recognised Da anywhere. Yes, his body had shrunk, and his face was bony and thin, but there was no denying this man was Thomas Rory O'Connor, Da.

Caleb reached out and gently touched his arm. "Da, wake up."

Da slowly opened his eyes, the whites no longer white, but yellow, like the rest of his body. He had trouble focussing, but his face lit up a little as he recognised Caleb.

"Caleb. Good to see you, son." He held out his thin arm to Caleb.

Caleb helped him to a sitting position and placed several pillows behind his back. Daniel was shocked at the tenderness his brother was showing Da. He would never have expected it.

But then, although this man looked like Da, the similarity ended there. This man was weak, his voice no more than a raspy whisper, not loud and churlish as Daniel remembered. Difficult to tie the two together.

"Da, I've brought someone with me." Caleb held Da's hand and glanced at Daniel.

"Who's that?" Da peered at Daniel, but there was no recognition on his face.

"It's Daniel, Da. Daniel's here."

Until that moment, Daniel could have turned and walked

away, but now it was too late. He had no choice. He had to face Da.

His chest tightened and he couldn't speak. His mouth wouldn't work. Gulping, he tried to steady his pounding heart.

Da sat straighter and peered at Daniel more intensely.

"Daniel, you say?" He glanced at Caleb and then back at Daniel.

"Yes, Da. It's Daniel." *Just as well Caleb could speak.*

"Ah, Daniel, my boy. Come here." Da reached out his hand, and Daniel had no choice but to take it.

Da's fingers were long, thin and bony. His grip, weak but warm. Daniel pushed back the tears that pricked the corners of his eyes.

"What a handsome boy you are. Come closer so I can take a better look at you."

Daniel obeyed and sat on the chair beside the bed.

"I never thought I'd see you again, son. This is a real surprise." The man's face softened into a grin, the warmth in his voice throwing Daniel.

How can this man be Da? Got to say something... but what?

DANIEL TOOK A DEEP BREATH. "DA..." His voice faltered. He gulped. Caleb's hand on his shoulder helped steady him.

"It's okay, son. I know it's a shock." Da patted his hand. "I've seen the light. I'm not the same man anymore."

Daniel blinked his eyes. This was too much to take. He didn't know this man, and he had no idea how to respond. Da was a drunkard. A bully. This man was neither.

God, please help me. This is too hard.

"Da, Daniel lives in England. He's married and has a little boy."

A faint smile grew on Da's face and his eyes lit up. "Is that right, son? You'll have to bring them in." He coughed and wheezed. "I'm sorry, son. This body, it's giving way on me." Another coughing bout interrupted them.

He didn't look good, that was for sure. *How long did Caleb say he had left?* Daniel recalled his words...

"If he doesn't get a liver transplant, he's probably only got three or four weeks..."

Not very long at all. But this wasn't Da. He didn't know this man. How could Da have changed that much?

"I'm glad you came, son." Da's breathing was slow and measured. "I don't deserve to see any of you. I was a terrible father." Another coughing bout interrupted him. "I'm truly sorry for the way I treated you and Mam." He struggled for breath, but continued anyway.

"I could blame the drink, but I won't." He paused, a far-away look in his eyes. Turning his head and looking directly at Daniel, he continued, "I was a bully, and the drink just made it worse. It's a pity I didn't see the light earlier, son. All those years, wasted." His eyes watered. Daniel gulped.

"You probably won't believe me when I say I'm sorry, son. And I don't blame you, but I am sorry. I don't deserve to be your Da."

Da was apologising? No way. Words like that could never come out of that drunkard's mouth. But it certainly sounded like it.

Daniel's heart thumped. Unable to move, let alone speak, he had to respond. But what would he say? *'It's okay, Da, what you did is forgiven and forgotten? Beating Mam until she couldn't move was nothing - it's okay?'* No, he wasn't ready to forgive and forget. Maybe he never would be. How could God ever expect him to do that?

"I'm sorry, I can't cope with this. I need to go." Daniel stood. Backing away, he cast another look at the emaciated stranger lying in the bed before fleeing for the sanctuary of the corridor.

What would Lizzy think? He'd let her down, but there was no way he'd let Da off that lightly. Da had destroyed their family, and now he says sorry, and it should be okay? *What a load of shite. 'Sorry God, I didn't mean that.'*

Daniel reached inside his pocket and took out a cigarette, ignoring the 'No Smoking' sign on the wall. His hands shook so much he had trouble lighting up. The first drag helped to calm him, and he inhaled slowly. He caught sight of Caleb coming out of the room and turned away. He'd let Caleb down too. He really was a failure.

"Hey there, Danny." Caleb placed his hand gently on Daniel's shoulder.

Daniel shrugged it off. "Just leave it, okay? I couldn't do it." He took another drag of his cigarette. "Let's get out of here."

"No problem, Danny."

So annoying how cool Caleb is about everything.

"Want to get a drink?"

Daniel shrugged. He couldn't care less. He'd blown it, and all he wanted to do was crawl into a hole and hide. Or punch someone. Da, probably. *That pathetic git of a man. How dare he apologise!*

Caleb started the car and drove a short distance before pulling up in front of a snack bar.

"This do?"

"Guess so." *A pub would be better.*

Daniel climbed out of the car and followed Caleb inside.

"What'll it be?" The young girl behind the counter stood waiting, chewing gum and looking bored.

"A chocolate milkshake and a pastie for me. How about you, Danny?"

He didn't care. But no use taking his frustration out on Caleb and this girl. Sighing, he pulled himself together.

"The same, thanks."

Daniel followed Caleb to a table in the corner of the shop. He leaned back and crossed his arms, staring at the grubby red and white plastic tablecloth.

"It was a shock, wasn't it, seeing him like that?"

Daniel glanced up and considered his reply. Not only had Da changed, but Caleb had too. It'd been a mistake coming back. He didn't know any of his family anymore. Lizzy and Dillon were his family now - he should be with them. But how could he face Lizzy? He'd failed. Let her down. Let God down. Let himself down.

He lowered his head and squeezed back the tears stinging his eyes. It was too much. Paul had told him to face his challenges head on, and to lean on God for strength and wisdom. He thought he'd tried. Maybe he hadn't truly let go. He'd been so determined to hate Da. But that's not what God wanted, of that Daniel was now certain. But it rankled so much. He clenched his fists. What right did Da have to come back and upend everything? That git's intrusion into his new life with

Lizzy and Dillon wasn't welcome. But it was real, and had to be faced. Daniel took a deep breath and looked up.

"Yes." Daniel held Caleb's gaze. "You warned me, but I didn't believe you. That man wasn't Da."

"You're right. He's not the Da we remember, that's for sure." Caleb lifted his gaze to the young girl placing the milkshakes and pasties on the table. "Thank you, love."

She smiled and walked away slowly, her hips swaggering a little too much.

"You'd better tell me about him. Now I've seen him for myself, I need to know how he got to be like that so I can try to understand." Daniel sat straighter in his seat.

"No problem." Caleb took a long suck of his milkshake. "After he left, he hit the grog pretty hard, and he can't remember much of those years. He lived on the streets mainly, and was in and out of rehab, but he always went back to the bottle." Caleb took another slurp before continuing. "About twelve months ago a street worker took an interest in him and convinced him to dry out for good. Not sure how it happened, but I guess Da was sick of his life, and agreed to go to the centre. They helped him get off the grog for good. He said it was the hardest thing he's ever done, and he almost gave in, but he's been off the drink now for almost a year. Sometime during all that, he found God."

Daniel shook his head and glanced out the window before looking back to Caleb. He narrowed his eyes and sighed.

"That's what I don't understand. How can a person who's lived a life like that, who beat his wife and kids, and has been a drunk all his life, suddenly say they've found God, and then everything's supposed to be okay?"

"That's exactly what Grace says. She won't accept he's changed. I keep telling her to check for herself, but she won't. But you saw him. He's different. You can't deny that."

No, Daniel couldn't deny Da was different. But it might be a put on. He didn't trust the man.

"I don't buy it. He was certainly different. But I reckon he could be faking it. He must want something."

Caleb shook his head. "I don't think he does. I've been seeing him now for a few months and haven't noticed anything to make me think he's pretending. He really does seem genuine."

"So we're supposed to say it's alright, and let him back into our lives, after all he did?"

Caleb took a deep breath and held Daniel's gaze.

"I can't tell you what you should do, Danny, but that's what I've done. As a Christian, I believe God wants me to do that. Especially since Da's asked for our forgiveness, and he seems to genuinely mean it. It'd be wrong of me to not forgive him."

That's exactly what Lizzy said I should do. Daniel sighed heavily.

"I'm not ready to forgive, Caleb. I'm sorry. Maybe because I'm a new Christian and I'm still learning, but it's all too quick. I don't see how a person can just say they're sorry and then get let off the hook for everything they've done."

"But isn't that what happened when we became Christians? We're all guilty of bad stuff, Danny, but God forgave us, regardless of what we'd done. There really isn't any difference. And besides, he's already paid a hefty price. He lost his family."

"But how do we know he means it?"

"We don't. Only God knows what's in a man's heart. But *we're* in the wrong if we don't forgive."

Caleb was right. But he couldn't do it. Not yet.

"I need a smoke."

Caleb pushed his chair back. "Let's take a walk along the river."

Strolling along the edge of the River Lagan, memories of when he and Colin came down here as lads flitted once again through Daniel's mind. Last he'd heard, Colin had left the estate and moved to the other side of town. Maybe he should look Colin up – shouldn't be that hard to find him.

"Just like old times, hey Danny?"

Daniel turned his head and caught Caleb's eyes before letting out a small chuckle.

"Yeah. Nothing much has changed." Daniel opened his cigarette packet and offered one to Caleb.

Caleb hesitated, but then took one. "Caity won't be happy." He leaned forward while Daniel lit it for him.

"Special occasion." A slow grin grew on Daniel's face.

Caleb chuckled, his whole face expanding into a beaming smile. "Yes, it is." He threw his arm around Daniel's shoulders.

"So what's it like being back?"

Daniel exhaled slowly, blowing puffs of smoke into the air.

"Strange. Very strange. Not sure what to make of it all, to be honest. Have you ever thought of leaving?"

"Nah. Too hard. And Caity wouldn't leave her family. Can't imagine living anywhere else."

"Don't know if I could move back. Too many memories." Daniel took a long drag on his cigarette and stared at the river.

A barge, laden with assorted drums, chugged slowly upstream towards the city docks.

"You've done good for yourself, Danny. Looks like you've landed on your feet. Lizzy's something special."

Daniel laughed and shook his head. "I'm still amazed she married me."

"Look after her, man. She's a good one."

"You're telling me? I almost lost her. I was an eejit. You know, I could've easily turned out like Da." Daniel gulped. The image of Da's emaciated body sent a shiver down his spine. Would have been him in years to come if God hadn't touched his life when He did. If only Da had 'seen the light' earlier.

A wave of pity floated over Daniel's heart and tugged at his conscience. Maybe he should go back and see Da. Daniel took a deep breath. *Tomorrow. Maybe.*

"Come on, man. Let's get back to our girls." Caleb clapped his hand on Daniel's back.

Daniel stubbed out his cigarette and nodded. God was at work, but would he have the strength to do what was being asked of him?

Passing a bin, Daniel took the packet of cigarettes from his pocket and threw it in. "There weren't many left anyway."

CHAPTER 8

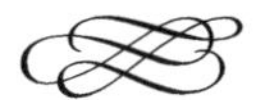

As Daniel entered the living room, Lizzy studied him carefully. Had it gone well? She'd hoped Daniel would be relaxed and happy, but he walked slowly, his shoulders sagging, and his eyes dull. Lizzy's heart fell. There it was again. She'd expected everything to be sorted straight away. *When would she learn?* Hadn't she prayed that God would let him go at his own speed?

Her heart ached for him. She walked towards him, and brushing the hair from his forehead with her fingertips, placed a gentle kiss on his lips.

"Are you okay?" Lizzy searched Daniel's eyes, trying to read what was going on inside him.

Daniel placed his hands on her hips and held her gaze.

"Getting there. Slowly." Pulling her close, he hugged her tightly. The tension in his body eased as she caressed his back with her fingertips.

"Thank you, Liz." He pulled away and held her at arm's

length. Her pulse quickened as he leaned forward and kissed her.

Caitlin appeared from the kitchen holding two mugs of steaming hot coffee.

"Oh, I'm sorry! Didn't mean to interrupt… just thought you might like these." She let out a small laugh as she placed the mugs on the coffee table.

"Thanks Caity." Lizzy smiled fondly, and then, after taking a deep breath to steady herself, moved away from Daniel and picked Dillon up from his bouncer.

"Any plans for the rest of the day?" Caleb asked of no-one in particular.

"We can catch a bus into town and show Lizzy the city." Caitlin pulled the curtain back and glanced out the window. "The weather's not too bad."

Lizzy looked at Daniel and lifted her eyebrow. Was it safe to wander around Belfast? Hadn't he said there was still trouble?

Daniel turned his head to Caitlin. "Sounds good, Caitlin, but Lizzy's worried about how safe it is."

Lizzy narrowed her eyes and glared at him. "Daniel! Thanks for that!"

Caitlin chuckled. "It's okay, Lizzy. Most people think that way. It's true. There are problem areas, and you do have to be careful, but generally, everyone just goes about their business as normal. Promise we'll bring you home in one piece."

Lizzy smiled, relieved offense hadn't been taken. "That would be nice, then. I'd like to see Belfast. Have I got time to feed Dillon?"

"Yes, go ahead. Easier to feed him here," Caitlin replied with another chuckle. "I'll get the girls ready while you sort him."

HALF AN HOUR LATER, the group stood at the bus stop at the end of the street. Lizzy's heart warmed at the sight of Daniel carrying Dillon in a pouch on his front. You couldn't ask for a more doting father. Daniel loved Dillon with all his heart. Almost too much, if that were possible. Memories of little baby Rachel must be floating through his mind now he was back here, near where he'd lived with her and Ciara all those years ago. Nessa said Daniel had doted on the baby girl too, but rarely since Dillon's birth had he mentioned her. Would he say anything about them? Would he point out the house where they lived? Would he want to visit their graves?

His mind must be a jumble of thoughts and memories. Lizzy took his hand as they sat together in the bus and leaned in close. She caught his eye and smiled. This trip was good for him. Confronting the past and letting go of all the hurt and sadness would free him to move forward if he allowed God in. She prayed he would, *but in his time, not mine...* That was the difficult bit.

If only the visit with his Da had gone better. But at least Daniel had said he might go back again tomorrow. That was promising. Warmth radiated through Lizzy's body, and she smiled to herself. Life was good. She gazed out the window and took in the run down area they were passing through. They'd had such different upbringings, she and Daniel. But it could have been so different. It was only Father's inheritance that had resulted in her being brought up with privilege. In fact, if he hadn't inherited, Father probably would have married Mathew's mother. What a strange thought! Really weird how things happen. How just a moment in time can change everything.

Lizzy's musings came to an abrupt end when the bus driver slammed on the brakes, throwing all the passengers forward in their seats. She held on tightly as the tyres squealed and the bus skidded out of control. Her heart thumped, waiting for the bus to come to a stop. When it did, the sound of shattering glass and passengers' screams sickened her. Throughout the bus, pandemonium reigned.

Her head hurt. She reached up and touched it. Must have hit the steel bar on the seat in front. A huge lump had appeared, but apart from that, she was okay. No broken bones or blood. She reached over to Daniel. Blood oozed from his head.

Lizzy's heart raced. "Daniel! Are you alright?" She wrapped her arms around him. *He has to be. How could this have happened?*

Daniel reached up slowly and felt his head. When he pulled his hand away, it was covered in blood.

"Here, take this. Hold it against your head." Lizzy handed him one of Dillon's nappies and helped him press it against his temple. Dillon was screaming. How he hadn't been hurt was a miracle. Daniel must have shielded him, but he wasn't responding now to Dillon at all. Daniel just sat, staring ahead in a daze. Lizzy helped him sit back in the seat and carefully extracted Dillon from the pouch.

"Oh my little man." Lizzy showered Dillon with kisses and tried to calm him. His little face was distraught. "It's okay, Dillon. There, there. We're safe." Lizzy cradled him in her arms and rocked him back and forth, gently caressing his head with her hand. Her heart raced, but she had to hold herself together for his sake.

In the few moments Lizzy had spent settling Dillon, Daniel had recovered and had moved forward to check on Caleb, Caitlin and the girls. Lizzy inched her way across the seat to reach them as well. Sirens wailing in the distance sent shivers through her body. Glass was strewn everywhere. She had to be careful. When she finally managed to pull herself forward, what she saw made her ill. The front of the bus had crumpled, and she couldn't see the passengers in the front seat. Tara and Imogen had been in those seats.

Caitlin crawled on hands and knees through the debris, trying to reach the girls. Lizzy's heart went out to her. She couldn't imagine the terror Caitlin would be feeling. Caleb was in front, Lizzy could just see his back. At least they were okay. *But what about the girls?*

"Daniel..." Lizzy held her hand out. When he turned, her eyes sought his. She needed his arms around her. He inched his way back and pulled her tight. She sobbed into his chest. "Thank you." Lizzy tilted her head and searched his eyes. "Are the girls okay?"

Daniel's eyes held grave concern. "I don't know, Liz. It doesn't look good."

Lizzy pushed back her tears, her stomach clenched with dread. She took a deep breath. "Let's go to them, Daniel." She glanced forward to Caitlin and Caleb who were both reaching into the space on the floor under the seat where Tara and Imogen had been sitting.

The wail from Caitlin sent chills through Lizzy's spine. *No,*

God. Please no. Let them be okay.

Lizzy grabbed Daniel's hand tighter as they made their way together through the debris strewn all around. Caitlin sat on the floor, reaching out to Imogen who lay on the floor under the seat, limp, lifeless and covered in blood. Caleb held Tara in his arms. Her eyes were open, but her face was bruised and bloody.

Lizzy bent down and wrapped her free arm around Caitlin's shoulders and prayed. "Oh God, be with Caity and precious little Imogen. Comfort her, I pray. Wrap them in Your arms. Oh God, please help them. Give them strength."

The wail of sirens stopped, and a woman in a blue uniform appeared. She moved Caitlin out of the way and reached for Imogen. The woman glanced back at her partner and yelled for oxygen. Gaining access, the paramedic felt for a pulse.

Lizzy reached for Caitlin's hand and gave it a gentle squeeze.

"Stay positive, Caity," Lizzy whispered into her ear. *Oh God, let Imogen be okay.*

The paramedic worked on Imogen as Lizzy held Caitlin tightly. Daniel reached down and took Dillon. Lizzy caught his eyes and unspoken words passed between them, memories of Daniel's near death experience so fresh in her mind. As the paramedics worked, time stood still as life and death hung in the balance.

All around, other passengers tried to escape the wrecked bus, some on their own and others with help, but for Lizzy and

Caitlin, the only thing they heard were the words of the paramedic, "She's going to be alright."

Caitlin sobbed into Lizzy's chest as tears welled in her own eyes. *Thank You God. Thank You.*

"WE'LL HAVE to take her to hospital, but she's going to be alright." The paramedic gave Caitlin a warm smile as she squeezed her arm. "Would you like to come?"

Caitlin nodded, her eyes glistening.

She tried to stand, but was unsteady. Daniel caught her before she fell. The door of the bus had crumpled. The only way out was through the front where the windscreen had shattered, leaving a gaping hole. Caitlin followed the paramedics who'd placed Imogen on a stretcher, and was helped out by several men who'd come to the rescue.

Police cars, ambulances and firetrucks surrounded the bus and the car it had collided with. Lizzy gulped as she looked at the crumpled mess. No-one could have survived.

A waiting ambulance whisked Caitlin and Imogen away, leaving Lizzy, Daniel and Caleb, standing, dazed and in shock, on the pavement. They were all attended to, with temporary bandages applied where necessary. A nearby cafe provided hot cups of tea.

Clinging to her daddy, Tara refused to allow anyone to look at her injuries.

"Come on Tara, it's okay. They just want to clean you up," Caleb said, but she hid her face in his neck and sobbed.

Lizzy stroked her head. "Tara, are you okay, sweetie?" Lizzy leaned in close and lifted Tara's chin. "Your mummy and sister are going to be alright, sweetheart. Is that what you're worried about?"

Tara nodded, her big brown eyes full of fear and uncertainty. Blood from her face had smudged Caleb's shirt. One of the cuts on her face looked quite deep.

"Will you let me clean your face?" Lizzy asked. "Make it all pretty again?"

Tara nodded slowly and allowed Lizzy to take her from her daddy. Lizzy sat down and placed Tara beside her. A paramedic handed Lizzy a swab, and Lizzy gently wiped the blood off Tara's face. She also picked out the small slithers of glass stuck in Tara's hair.

"Show me your hands, sweetie." Tara reluctantly opened her hands and Lizzy cleaned them with a fresh swab. "There you are princess. All clean!"

Tara lifted her head, her big brown eyes melting Lizzy's heart. Lizzy forced back the tears pricking her eyes and gave Tara a gentle squeeze. Dillon had settled, and Daniel appeared unharmed now his cut was bandaged. Caleb, too, appeared to have escaped unharmed. Such a miracle.

As Lizzy stood, her head spun and she broke out in a sweat. Without any warning, she vomited on the road. She couldn't breathe. Daniel was talking, but his voice came to her as if through a tunnel.

His arms were around her, warm, safe and strong, and then a blanket was placed over her, but she was cold, oh so cold, and she couldn't stop shivering. *So sick... God, what's happening?*

The next thing Lizzy was aware of was being sat up and having her blood pressure taken. Everything was hazy. It was still daylight, and people still scurried around.

She grabbed Daniel's hand and looked into his eyes. Her breathing had steadied. "What happened, Daniel?"

"You went into shock, Lizzy." Daniel gently brushed her hair with his hand, his eyes filled with love and concern.

"Oh..." Lizzy leaned her head on his shoulder and gazed around. Slowly, it all came back. She bolted upright, her heart thumping.

"Tara. Where's Tara?"

"She's with Caleb, just beside you. She's okay, Lizzy, no need to worry. Here my darling, take a sip." Daniel held a cup to her lips. The hot sweet liquid slid down her throat, warming, calming.

"I don't believe that happened. I feel so embarrassed, Daniel."

"Don't be, Liz. We've all had a shock." Daniel hugged her gently as she leaned against him.

Lizzy reached for Dillon and rocked him in her arms, her heart breaking with love for him. What would she have done if something had happened to him? No, she couldn't even think about that.

In Lizzy's arms, Dillon squealed and kicked. Lizzy fought back tears as she rocked him. The more she relaxed, the calmer he became. So much a part of her. She kissed the top of his head and closed her eyes, calm settling deep in her soul. *Thank You so much God for looking after us all.*

"Dillon's fine, Liz," Daniel said, pulling her close. "We're all fine."

Lizzy lifted her head, searching his eyes. "Yes, we are." She drew in a deep breath. "I pray Imogen pulls through." Tears pricked her eyes.

"She's in good hands, Lizzy."

"Yes." Lizzy straightened herself. "I feel very thankful, Daniel. It could have been so much worse. If I'd lost either of you after all we've been through..."

"Hush, Lizzy." He kissed her cheek and pulled her closer.

Sitting there on the pavement, wrapped in Daniel's arms, and surrounded by what could only be described as a disaster zone, Lizzy wondered at the irony of it all. Only a short while ago she'd been worried about walking around Belfast for fear of being bombed, but here they were, lucky to be alive after a traffic accident. She snuggled closer to Daniel. Life was so precious and unpredictable. Her heart filled with love for her husband and little boy, and for God who had brought them together and had kept them safe.

LIZZY LOOKED up as a young red-headed paramedic bent down.

"You worried us there for a second." He took her arm and checked her pulse.

"I feel fine now." Lizzy gave him a warm smile as she straightened herself.

"You seem okay, but you both need to get checked out properly, just in case."

The paramedic stood and reached out a hand to help Daniel up.

"Thank you. We will." Daniel helped Lizzy to stand, quickly placing his arm around her when she wobbled.

"You can go to hospital in an ambulance, but you'll need to wait, unless you can get there by yourselves..."

"We'll be right." Caleb appeared with Tara still clinging to him. "I've just called my sister - she'll be here shortly."

WITHIN MINUTES, Grace pulled up in her red sports car. All eyes turned towards her as her long shapely legs peeled out of the tiny car. Elegantly dressed in a navy blue designer suit with stilettos to match and her make-up and hair coiffed perfectly, she looked very much out of place amongst the mayhem.

Her eyes widened as she surveyed the scene. Stepping around the glass and other debris scattered everywhere, Grace headed straight for the small family group huddled together on the pavement. She stopped in front of Caleb and wrapped her arms around him and Tara.

"Thank goodness you're alright." Grace's voice faltered and she brushed tears from her eyes.

She straightened, and then turned to Daniel, hugging him tightly.

"This is terrible, Danny. Are you okay?" Her eyes went straight to the cut on his forehead.

"Yes, I'm fine, thanks, Grace." He smiled appreciatively.

"Come on, let's get you to hospital." Grace ushered them all towards her car.

"We're not all going to fit. Take Caleb and Tara first, Grace - there's no hurry for us," Daniel said, taking Lizzy's hand.

Caleb gave Daniel a bear hug and clung a little longer than normal. Caleb's hands shook and his eyes twitched. *He must be so worried about Imogen...*

"Thanks Danny." Caleb let go of Daniel and then walked towards the car with Tara still in his arms.

"We'll be praying for you..." Lizzy called out as they reached the car. Her voice caught in her throat, and her eyes filled with tears.

As Caleb turned and caught her gaze, his pinched face made her gulp. *What if Imogen doesn't make it?*

Daniel placed his arm around Lizzy's shoulder as the sports car roared off. She leaned in to him. "He must be so worried, Daniel."

~

LEFT ALONE, Daniel and Lizzy sat on the pavement clinging to each other. What if he'd lost her? He couldn't imagine life without Lizzy now, after everything they'd been through. Daniel's heart hurt with love for her. Lizzy, the most precious thing to come into his life, ever. Lizzy, his best friend, his lover, his companion. *No way do I deserve her, but oh God, I'm so thankful You brought her into my life.*

Deep in Daniel's soul, an overwhelming ache grew. God had done so much for him, and once again, he'd failed. What kind of person walks out on their own father, especially on his death bed? Da had been so humble and honest, so different to what Daniel had expected.

But I threw it all in his face. I rejected his plea for forgiveness. How could I have done that? What kind of person am I?

A hard lump formed in his throat, and a wave of nausea rose from within. His breath came fast and hard, he shivered, but sweat beads formed on his forehead. He let go of Lizzy's hand. He'd never felt so sick in his life. Not even when he'd been drunk. But it wasn't physical sickness - his soul was ill.

Daniel hung his head between his knees as sobs racked his body. *Oh God, I'm so sorry. I'm sorry... please forgive me...*

Lizzy placed her arm over him and held him. He was so ashamed... *how could I have done that? God forgave me for everything, and so has Lizzy. She didn't need to. She could have just left me in a heap. That's what I deserved. And yet, she stood by me, nursed me, loved me when I didn't deserve it. Despite all the love and forgiveness shown to me, I couldn't forgive my own Da. What a pathetic person I am.*

Oh God... what have I done? More heart wrenching sobs tore through Daniel's body. Lizzy's arms tightened around him. His chest heaved. *Need to make this right, God... please help me.*

Resting in Lizzy's arms, Daniel's breathing slowly steadied. He knew what he had to do.

Daniel gulped and inhaled deeply before lifting his head. He gazed into Lizzy's eyes.

"I'm so sorry, Liz."

"Daniel, it's alright." Her eyes glistened with tears as she ran her fingers down his cheek.

"I'm not sure what happened... it all just hit me ... Da, you, this accident..."

"Shh, my love, it's okay." Lizzy pulled him close and rocked him like a baby. He clung to her.

"I love you, Liz. With all my heart, I love you."

"I know that Daniel. I love you with all my heart, too." She pulled him closer and there he remained, cocooned in Lizzy's arms until Dillon interrupted, demanding attention.

"Are you okay, Daniel?" Lizzy asked as she straightened herself and sat Dillon on her lap.

Daniel took a moment as he considered his reply. Yes, he

was okay. Inside he was calmer, and confident that God would give him the strength to do what needed to be done.

He nodded slowly as Grace's car turned the corner and came to a halt beside them.

As Grace slid out and closed the door, Daniel drew in a deep breath. In those few minutes, God had done something deep inside him, and as he looked at Grace, dressed to impress, beautiful, intelligent and world-wise, his heart went out to her. *Yes, she might appear to have everything, Lord, but she needs You. Just like I need You.*

Before he made a move, Daniel squeezed Lizzy's hand and caught her eye. They were in this together, and God was with them. And for that, he was eternally grateful.

CHAPTER 9

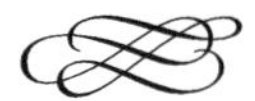

"You really have done alright, sis," Daniel said as he and Lizzy entered Grace's apartment on the fourth floor of an ultra-sleek complex not far from the city centre. Through the expansive glass sliding doors leading out to a large balcony, the city sprawled into the distance. On the inside, the living room was furnished elegantly, but was clinical, like a hotel room, not a home. Everything was modern and crisp, but lacked any warmth or personal touch. The lone photograph on a shelf in the kitchen of Caleb, Caitlin and the two girls was the only indication a real person lived here.

"I've worked jolly hard, and it's mortgaged to the hilt." Grace placed her handbag on the marble kitchen bench and turned the kettle on. "What can I get you?"

"Just a cup of tea, thanks Grace. I'm still feeling a little off," Lizzy said, handing Dillon back to Daniel. "May I use your bathroom?"

"Of course, Lizzy. Just through here." Grace showed Lizzy to the bathroom, and then returned to the kitchen.

"I wish she'd stayed in overnight," Daniel said quietly. "Lizzy's so stubborn sometimes."

"I'm sure if they were worried they would've made her stay."

Daniel sighed heavily. "Guess so, but I'm still worried." He lifted Dillon onto his shoulder and rubbed the baby's back.

"How did your visit go with Da?" Grace took three china mugs from the shelf above the bench and placed them in front of her before settling her gaze on Daniel's. Her eyes held a smirk that churned his stomach.

The question he'd been dreading… Daniel pulled a stool from under the bench and sat, pondering how best to reply. How could he admit he'd stomped out when he wanted to be a witness of God's love to Grace? What would she think of him? *If only I'd been prepared to forgive Da this morning…* Sighing deeply, Daniel tried to steady the thoughts swirling in his head. *Lord God, what do I tell her?*

The truth...

Daniel gulped. Where had that come from? *The truth?* Daniel took a deep slow breath and held Grace's gaze. He had to answer. An empty feeling grew in the pit of his stomach. *God, You need to give me the words...*

His heart pounded. *Okay, here goes...* He swallowed hard. "I have to be honest, Grace, I didn't handle it too well." Daniel shifted in his seat. "Caleb had warned me about what to expect, but I wasn't prepared." He paused, holding her gaze. "Grace, you might not believe this, but Da apologised."

"I wouldn't believe a word that came out of that decrepit

man's mouth." Grace spat the words with such vehemence it threw Daniel. His eyebrows furrowed. What was going on? Had something else happened he wasn't aware of?

"Yes, well, I didn't believe him either. I couldn't tie together the man we knew as Da, and the man lying in that bed." Daniel closed his eyes tightly, and pulled his mind from the past to the present.

Shifting in his seat, Daniel rocked Dillon in his arms. The baby was restless and had started to whimper. *Come on, Lizzy...*

He lifted his head and looked straight into Grace's eyes. "I couldn't handle it, Grace, and I raced out of the room without speaking to him." Daniel's voice caught in his throat. "I feel so ashamed." He paused and inhaled deeply. "I've had time to think, though, and I've decided to go back tomorrow and make it right." He gulped. There, he'd said it...

Grace rolled her eyes and shook her head. "Don't tell me Caleb's been in your ear with all his religious nonsense. He's gone soft, he has."

Daniel slumped a little on his stool. "What's happened to you, Grace? You never used to be so cynical." His heart went out to her. She'd been hurt, that was obvious. *But will she talk to me?*

Their eyes locked. Daniel held his breath.

"Just...things."

"Like what? You can talk to me, Grace. You know that."

Grace busied herself with making tea.

Daniel reached out his hand and grabbed her arm. As she lifted her eyes, a lone tear rolled down her cheek. He reached out and pulled her towards him as Lizzy reappeared. Grace quickly wiped the tear away and patted her hair before turning to face Lizzy as if nothing had happened.

"Feel better?" The smile planted on Grace's face was too cheerful.

"Yes, thanks. I couldn't believe what a wreck I looked." Lizzy let out a small laugh as she took Dillon from Daniel's arms.

Had she noticed Grace's tears?

"There, there, little man. Look at you! You need some cleaning up too if that smell's anything to go by." Lizzy sat on the leather couch, placing Dillon on her lap. "Is it okay to change him here, Grace, or would you rather somewhere else?"

"There's fine, Lizzy. No problem."

"What kind of law do you practice, Grace?" Daniel asked, settling back on his stool. A change of topic was needed.

"I work for the Prosecutor's Office as a junior barrister."

"You'd be good at that." Daniel let out a small chuckle and smiled teasingly at Grace. He wouldn't like to be prosecuted by her, that was for sure.

"I do alright. Should make senior barrister in the next year or so."

"Never thought of changing sides?"

Grace gave a mirthless laugh. "And what, help all those criminals get off? No way."

"Hit a touchy point there..."

Grace shot him a wry look and placed her mug on the bench.

"You wouldn't believe the cases that come through. Some sick people out there."

"I know. But some of them just need help. Like me." Daniel

gulped as the memory of his most recent court appearance flashed through his mind. "I have no doubt I'd be in jail right now if it wasn't for my lawyer. Instead, I got put on probation and landed this amazing job. It was a real answer to prayer, wasn't it, Lizzy?"

Lizzy nodded and smiled, her eyes lighting up.

Grace sighed and shook her head in disgust. "How do you believe all that nonsense, Daniel? God doesn't answer prayer. Doubt he even exists."

Daniel let out a nervous laugh. "I know what you mean, Grace. I didn't think He existed until recently, but now, I know He does. I know it in here," Daniel said, placing his hand on his chest. His heart raced - he was completely out of his depth, but God was giving him the words, and he really did mean them. *If only Grace could see that.*

"Seems to me like religion has a lot to answer for. If God exists, why hasn't he stopped all the fighting?"

"That's the same question I asked for years. Lizzy helped me understand, didn't you, my love?"

Lizzy stood and joined Daniel and Grace, slipping her free arm around Daniel's waist.

"Yes, but it took a while. Not until you were ready to listen. Before then, it wouldn't have mattered what I'd said, you wouldn't have believed it." Lizzy's voice was calm and steady, and her eyes held warmth and sincerity.

"So what about our Da? Caleb says he's found God too." Grace narrowed her eyes. "Seems to me it's just a crutch for people to lean on when they can't sort themselves out." Grace faced Lizzy, her eyes widening as she reached out her hand and touched Lizzy lightly on the arm. "I didn't mean you,

Lizzy. Sorry. But people like our Da, and even Caleb and Danny with their drink problems. They should be able to sort themselves out without leaning on a God that probably doesn't exist. I think they're just fooling themselves." Grace leaned against the bench and folded her arms.

"Everyone's entitled to their own view, Grace." Lizzy took a stool beside her. "But for many, faith in God is real, and it changes their lives. It's just unfortunate that religion has given God a bad name, and turned a lot of people away from seeing the real God. But nobody can force anyone else to believe." Lizzy lifted Dillon onto her shoulder and gently patted his back.

How does she talk so calmly?

"Believing comes from an open heart, Grace, and a desire for truth. Then, and only then, does everything start to make sense and God can be seen for who He really is." Lizzy's eyes lit up. "A God who's real, and loving and caring. But He never forces Himself on anyone. It's a personal choice, and religion has nothing to do with it."

Lizzy reached out and squeezed Grace's hand. "Sorry if I've preached to you, Grace - I didn't mean to come over like that." Lizzy's smile was genuine and warm. If Grace couldn't see that Lizzy really meant what she said, his sister really must have blinkers on.

Grace remained silent, seemingly lost for words. She picked up her mug and took a sip before replying.

"It's okay, Lizzy. You're right, I've just been turned off religion by all I've seen, even from when I was little and our Da would come home drunk and beat Mam. Mam believed, but look what good it did her." Grace's breathing quickened. "Our

Da basically killed her. And all the religious hypocrites make me sick. I guess I've turned my back on religion and God, as I can't see that any good has ever come of it." She paused and steadied herself, then looked firstly at Lizzy, and then at Daniel. "But I do sense something different in you two. You seem genuine, Danny, but I'm not ready to even consider it. And don't ask me to go see our Da with you. I won't go."

Daniel chuckled. His sister was fiery, that was for sure. "Don't worry, sis, I won't."

"Good." Grace collected the empty mugs and placed them in the sink. "We'd better check if Caleb and Caitlin are ready to be picked up," she said, effectively changing the topic as she wiped the bench and tidied everything away.

~

GRACE COLLECTED Caleb and Tara from the hospital and dropped them at their home so Caleb could get his car. Imogen's injuries weren't life threatening, but the doctors wanted her to stay in hospital overnight, so Caleb planned to return with a change of clothes for both Caitlin and Imogen.

On her way back, Grace briefly stopped in at the Prosecutor's Office to tell them she wouldn't be back in that day, and possibly even the next. She had so much work to do, but needed to spend time with her family, especially after this accident. Grabbing some files, she squeezed them into her briefcase. She'd stay up all night if needed. Sleep was overrated.

The accident, though unfortunate, had provided more time to spend with Daniel and Lizzy. Such an odd couple, but somehow it worked. She could probably enjoy their company, *but not if they begin preaching.* Lizzy's words had touched a chord, but Grace didn't want to go there. She had everything she needed. A good job where she was highly in demand, her apartment and car, a few good friends, and enough money to do whatever she wanted. She lacked nothing, not even male company. Any number of young men were at her beck and call, and she did occasionally call, but not often. It didn't pay to let any of them think they had a chance. After her one serious relationship had ended badly, she now kept any interested men at arm's length.

Grace pulled up outside the local store to grab some supplies - she'd have to play hostess with Caitlin out of action, and she wasn't prepared. Most nights Grace would grab a take-out meal on the way home from work, or eat at her desk. By the time she finished each night, she was in no mood to cook. Besides, she didn't know how.

Entering the store, Grace grabbed a trolley and began to walk the aisles. *What do you feed your siblings and their partners? Meat and veg? Frozen pizza?* The more she looked, the more confused she became. She picked up some frozen meals and then promptly put them back. *Party pies, sausage rolls, frozen pasties....?* Her pulse quickened. *Have to get something...* After ten minutes, all her trolley held were drinks and crisps. *I can't do this.* She glanced at her watch. *Too long already - have to order in.* Her heart rate immediately steadied as she strode to the checkout.

"Having a party, love?" The middle aged woman behind the register glanced quickly at Grace as she rang through the bottles of Coca Cola and Fanta and the packets of crisps and sweets Grace had piled up.

"Kind of. Just a family gathering." Grace fidgeted with her purse and took out enough cash to pay the woman. She couldn't wait to get out of there. Reaching the car, Grace placed the bags on the front seat before climbing in and speeding off. She'd never get sick of the sound of her sports car, nor the heads it turned. She'd never fit into a normal life. Ever.

Moments later, Grace pulled up in the underground car park and headed upstairs, hesitating a moment to steady herself before opening the door. She'd need her wits if any of them started talking about God again. She steeled herself and opened the door.

"Grace, here, let me help with that." Daniel jumped up and took the bags out of Grace's hands as she struggled to get in.

"Thanks Danny." She'd half expected to see Aislin and Alana there, but breathed with relief when they weren't. Not that she didn't like them - she hardly knew them, but she wanted to spend more time with Danny & Lizzy. Something about the couple intrigued her. Maybe it was how well they got on. Rarely had she seen a relationship that worked, and where both partners were happy, but Daniel and Lizzy really seemed to like each other. Grace smiled to herself. Yes, that was it - they actually liked each other! And it was contagious. She felt immediately happier around them, even if they did talk about God. She'd just have to overlook that for now.

"Aislin and Alana not here?" Grace asked Daniel as she began to unpack the bags.

"No, just us. Lizzy's having a lie down with Dillon - the accident took it out of her. She's still feeling a little shaken."

"Maybe she should go back to the hospital."

"She won't go." Daniel pinched his lips together.

Grace stopped unpacking and leaned back against the bench, folding her arms. "I really like Lizzy. Make sure you look after her, Daniel."

"Planning on it, sis. Learned my lesson big time, and I'm not going to blow it."

"Glad to hear it." Grace gave a soft laugh. "Let's grab a drink and have a chat before everyone gets here. I'm going to have a gin and tonic... oh dear, maybe that's not a good choice, and I should just have coke."

"It's okay, Grace. If you want a G and T, have one. I'm learning to deal with it. Can't allow my problem with drink to affect everyone else."

"You sure?"

"Have what you want, Grace, it really is okay. But I'll have coke."

Leaning forward, Grace kissed him on the cheek. "Proud of you, Danny. If only our Da had your strength when he was younger." Lowering her eyes, Grace pushed down the growing ache in her chest. "Everything would have been so different if he hadn't drunk." Grace's voice caught, and tears stung her eyes. *Again.* Quickly turning, she grabbed some glasses from the shelf above as she tried to regain control.

"Grace, what's the matter? Look at me." As Daniel placed his hand gently on her shoulder and turned her slowly to face him, she fought hard to push back the unwanted tears.

"It's nothing. Really Danny, it's nothing." Grace stood stiffly and turned her head away, wiping her face with the back of her hand. *Drat Daniel for having this effect.* She hadn't shed this many tears in years, but just being with him revived memories she'd shoved to the back of her mind, never to be thought of again. But now they threatened to be her undoing.

As Daniel wrapped his arms around her, she lost control and convulsions racked her body. Her eyes burned from tears she'd refused to shed until now.

Daniel held her tight. "Grace, whatever it is, it's okay," he whispered quietly as she continued to sob uncontrollably.

Grace nodded, but it wasn't okay. *How can it ever be okay?* The ache in her heart wouldn't leave. But she could never talk about it. Aunt Hilda had made her promise. Had threatened her…

Drat you Daniel. Drat you! She pounded his chest.

Daniel grabbed her hands. "Whoa Grace! What's going on?"

She raised her head slightly. "Nothing."

"Right."

Grace slowly straightened and pulled herself together, wiping her face with a tissue Daniel gave her.

Daniel pulled back and lifted her chin. She avoided his eyes.

"If you don't want to talk about it now, Grace, it's fine. Lizzy and I are here for you, whenever you're ready, okay?"

Grace shrugged and turned her head. Her insides churned and her head hurt. *I'll never talk about it.*

She closed her eyes and inhaled deeply. Never again would she let this happen.

MOVING AWAY FROM DANIEL, Grace headed straight for the drinks' cabinet and took out the bottle of gin. With her back to Daniel, she poured a measure, and then just a little more, before adding the tonic.

Daniel had grabbed a coke and was seated on the sofa. "Come on, Grace, come and join me." He held his hand out, his eyes soft and caring. How was she supposed to hold it together? No, she needed space.

"Come outside, Danny." Out there she could hide.

Leaning on the railing, Grace concentrated on the city lights. Breathing in the cool night air, she allowed the G and T to do its job. She had to regain control. She refused to let the others see her like this. The hardened, cool-headed lawyer no-one got close to, a blubbering mess? No. No-one would see her like that.

THE DOORBELL RANG. Grace downed the last of her drink and walked inside, pausing in front of the hallway mirror. Her face had lost its flush, but her eyes were still slightly puffy and red. No time for eye drops, she'd just have to get by. Lifting her chin, she took a deep breath before opening the door.

"There you are!" She flashed a warm smile at Caleb and Tara. "I was beginning to wonder where you were!" She inched back to let them through.

"Took a bit longer than planned, sorry Grace. Immi didn't want Tara to leave and I had to tear her away. Was a bit awkward."

"I should have brought Tara back with me. Sorry Caleb - I didn't think..." Grace looked up at Caleb apologetically before bending down and giving Tara a cuddle. It was true - she didn't think often enough when it came to things like that.

"No problem, Grace."

A moment later Lizzy reappeared with Dillon in her arms.

"Feel better, sweetie?" Daniel asked, reaching out for Dillon.

"Heaps, but my neck's a bit sore." Lizzy rubbed her neck and moved her head from side to side.

"Hope it's not whiplash, Lizzy," Grace said, standing up and joining her. "Might be best to get it checked."

"You may be right. I'll see how it is in the morning."

The doorbell rang again. This time it was Aislin and Alana, without their partners who'd been conveniently delayed at work. Although she felt a little guilty, Grace was relieved they hadn't come.

"Come in girls. Good to see you." Grace hugged each girl in turn and then offered them a drink.

Now they were all here, she'd take control and ensure her walls stayed up. Because that's what she did. Even with family.

~

DANIEL KEPT an eye on Grace all night. The small peek she'd allowed him into her real self had been unsettling. He'd seen an inkling the previous night, but he'd put most of that down to the excitement of meeting up again after all this time, not something deeper inside. Out of all his siblings, Grace had been his favourite. Sure, he and Caleb were close, and often it'd been left to them as the two eldest to do all the things Da should have done, but it was Grace he'd had the most connection with. They understood each other, even as children.

Daniel looked at her now. Talking with Lizzy, Aislin and Alana, Grace was confident and in control. Not an inkling of the breakdown he'd witnessed earlier in the evening. His heart ached for her. *Grace, what's going on?*

Soon after, Caleb suggested they call it a night. Daniel was last out, and hung back to have a word with Grace.

"I'm going to see Da again tomorrow. Come with me, Grace. " He took her hand and held her gaze.

Grace shook her head, her lip twisting into a sardonic smile. "Sorry to let you down, big brother, but there's no way I'll ever see that man."

Daniel held up his hands. "Sorry - just thought I'd ask. Don't get all snarly."

Leaning forward, Daniel placed his hands gently on Grace's shoulders. "Grace, don't let whatever the problem is destroy you. Something's causing you pain. I don't have all the answers, but I know Someone who does, so please talk to me when you feel able."

Grace's eyes welled. Daniel pulled her close. "Promise me?"

Grace held herself erect and didn't respond.

Lying in bed that night, Daniel held Lizzy tightly. His body craved sleep, but his mind was once again active. His heart ached for Grace. It must have been horrible to be sent away as a young child. They'd never talked about how they all felt when Mam died. It wasn't the done thing. With no parents to care for them, they'd been told to be grateful they had family willing to take them in. They could have all been sent to a children's home. *Might've been better if we had...*

Daniel knew how he coped. He'd turned to drink. What had Grace done to survive those years? What had happened to her heart and mind? A twelve year old girl needed her mother. Had Aunt Hilda understood that and helped her, or had she just told Grace to 'get on', the most common way local folk had of dealing with life? Would she ever let her guard down long enough to allow him, or anyone else, into her tightly walled life? Would she open her heart to God's love and healing?

Daniel nuzzled Lizzy's neck. "We need to pray for Grace."

"Mmm. Yes, we do." Yawning, Lizzy wriggled and stretched, then pulled herself up slowly and turned on the bedside lamp. "You really feel for her, don't you, Daniel?"

"I do, Lizzy. I've never felt like this before. It's like God's opened the eyes of my heart, and I can feel her hurt. I just want to help her, Liz."

Lizzy squeezed his hand. "I know. And I think it's wonderful. God's working in your life, Daniel, I see it with my own eyes, and it makes me so happy."

Daniel pulled her close and kissed the top of her head as she leaned into him.

"I'm sure He'll use you to help bring Grace to Himself, when she's ready," Lizzy said, peering into his eyes.

Daniel slumped and let out a slow breath.

"I know, but I want her ready now."

Lizzy chuckled quietly.

"I know what that's like!"

"Let's pray for her, Liz."

They joined hands and prayed that the Holy Spirit would soften Grace's heart and that she'd be open to God's healing touch. They prayed she'd hand over all the hurt from the past to Him, and learn to live in the freedom of new life in Jesus.

Lizzy hugged Daniel and wiped the tears rolling down his cheeks with a tissue.

"What about your Da, Daniel? Are you going to see him again?"

Daniel leaned back and took a deep breath.

"Yes, I am, Liz. God's been pricking my conscience all day, ever since I walked out of his room. I think I'm ready to forgive him." Daniel gulped. Never had he expected to hear those words come out of his mouth. "I've finally understood what you and Paul have been telling me all along. That absolutely everyone's a sinner, and that no-one deserves God's forgiveness. And that it doesn't matter how old they are, what they've done, what their life was like before, God's love and forgiveness is open to them. So, if Da has asked for my forgiveness, I need to let go of the hate I have for him, and try to see him as God does. A sinner, just like me, who's been forgiven. I don't think it'll be easy, but I'm prepared to try. It hit me today when I was talking with Caleb, that Da's already paid for all the bad things he did. He lost his family, and he lost his health. He basically lost his whole life."

Daniel turned his head and gazed into Lizzy's eyes.

"I'm so glad you stood by me, Liz, and that you didn't give up on me. If I'd lost you, I think I would have killed myself. But because of you, I've got new life in Jesus, and I've got the most beautiful wife and son a man could ever wish for."

Lizzy wrapped her arms around Daniel and held him. His body relaxed, and now he'd finally made the decision, he felt at peace with himself and with God.

CHAPTER 10

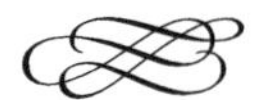

Daniel stirred in his sleep. *Was someone calling?* He turned over. Must be dreaming.

"Daniel." There it was again. Someone was calling out and knocking on the door.

Daniel sat up, immediately alert. *Caleb, and he sounds distressed.* Lizzy stirred. He peered at the bedside clock. Five am. What was Caleb doing, waking him so early? Dillon wasn't even awake yet.

Slipping out of bed, Daniel pulled on his robe and tiptoed to the door, opening it quietly before slipping out.

Caleb stood in the hallway, rubbing his arms and bouncing on his feet.

"What's up, Caleb?" Daniel whispered, pulling his robe tighter.

"The hospital just called. Da's body's shutting down." Caleb's voice faltered, and his face, in the pale pre-dawn light, was ashen.

Daniel felt faint. *No! This can't be happening.* Not now, not when he'd just made up his mind to see Da. *God, what are You doing?*

"Did they say how long he has?"

"No, but they said to come quickly, so it mustn't be long."

"We'd better go then. I'll tell Lizzy - she can stay with Tara."

Daniel crept back into the bedroom, trying not to disturb Dillon, and gently shook Lizzy.

Lizzy's eyes snapped open, and she pulled herself up, grabbing Daniel's arm.

"What's the matter, Daniel? Is Dillon okay?"

"Yes, it's not Dillon - it's Da."

Lizzy's eyes widened.

"Is he…?"

"No, but the hospital said to come quickly." Daniel forced down the lump in his throat. "Are you okay to mind Tara? We'll call as soon as we know anything."

"Sure, sweetie." She squeezed his arm. "Are you alright, Daniel?"

"I'm not sure. If anything happens and I don't get to speak to him, I don't know what I'll do." Daniel raked a hand through his hair. "I need to go, Liz." He quickly threw on his jeans and a clean T-shirt. Grabbing his jacket, he leaned over and kissed Lizzy gently on the top of her head.

She reached for his hand and looked up as he stood. "I'll be praying for you both."

Her words tugged at his heart.

"Thanks…" Daniel's voice trembled. He swallowed hard as he bent over and touched Dillon's cheek with his back of his hand. The baby had stirred and opened his eyes. Love for his little son flooded through Daniel. Had Da ever looked at him this way? *Unlikely.*

He kissed Lizzy again and then joined Caleb downstairs. Caleb looked as distressed as Daniel felt. How could he be feeling this way about a man who until yesterday he hadn't seen for almost twenty years, and who he'd only held bitterness and hate for? Now, with the very real possibility Da might die before they got there, a deep sense of loss already sat heavily on his soul.

"Come on man, let's go." Caleb pulled Daniel out of his thoughts and opened the door. Exiting quickly to stop the chill of the early morning air creeping inside, Daniel pulled the door closed and followed Caleb to the car. Caleb pumped the pedal several times before turning the ignition. The Escort sprang to life, the sound of the engine reviving memories of his and Lizzy's Escort. The one he wrecked. Daniel gulped and closed his eyes. It was all too much. *God, I don't know how to handle this.*

Caleb manoeuvred out of the tight car park before heading off down the street shrouded in semi-darkness.

"Planned on seeing him today." Daniel glanced at Caleb before returning his gaze to the slow moving traffic ahead, the red tail lights barely visible through the heavy fog.

"Thought you might. Bad timing, hey?"

Daniel slumped in his seat and sighed. "Yeah, could say that." He lifted his head. "Can he get a new liver?"

Caleb stared straight ahead and gripped the steering wheel tighter. "Doesn't want one."

Daniel's head jerked up. "What? He doesn't want one? Why not?"

Caleb sucked in a breath. "Said he doesn't deserve one."

Unbelievable...

Daniel balled his fists and tried to control the anger growing inside him. How could Da do that! Come into his life out of the blue, and then just disappear without a fight. *It's not on, Da. It's not on.* He pulled himself up and drew in a deep breath.

"We've got to get him one, Caleb."

Caleb shook his head. "He's already told the hospital he doesn't want one, so fat chance they'd go against his wishes, even if there was one to be had."

Daniel inhaled deeply. No use getting angry. He had to control himself.

"The best thing is to be there if he comes to."

Caleb was right, but Daniel wanted more. Now he'd decided to let Da back into his life, he wanted to spend time with him. Get to know him. Not say goodbye. *This wasn't meant to happen.*

The lights changed to green and Caleb let out the clutch. The car lurched forward and then took off as he pressed down heavily on the accelerator. The car had seen better days.

"Hope we get there in time." Daniel stared straight ahead. "Should we call Grace?"

Caleb glanced at Daniel and let out a heavy sigh.

"She won't come, but we can let her know. Aislin and Alana might. We'll call as soon as we get there." Caleb slowed down to take a left-hand corner. "I'll need to check on Caity and Immi too."

"At least they're in the same hospital."

"Yeah, that's a plus."

The hospital loomed ahead, stretching as far as the eye could see. Caleb parked, and he and Daniel strode to the main entrance where they checked the directory. Da was in the second last building on the right. They marched down the corridor, and reaching the end of that building, followed the path to the Intensive Care ward.

A short cheery nurse with a round face looked up.

"Can I help you?"

"We're looking for Thomas O'Connor." Caleb's voice faltered.

"Ah - Mr O'Connor. Down the corridor, third bed on the right. Go ahead - I'll check if the doctor's around."

"Thank you. How is he?"

"Not good, I'm sorry. He's had a few lucid moments, but I'll let the doctor fill you in."

Daniel's heart raced. He had to be there if Da came to. Striding ahead of Caleb, he found the bed. Faded blue curtains had been drawn to provide privacy. He took a deep breath, and finding the join in the curtains, he carefully pulled them apart and entered slowly, closing them behind him. There lay Da, just a skeleton of a man. Daniel swallowed hard.

"Da..." Daniel's voice was just a whisper. Seated on the plastic seat beside the bed, Daniel took one of Da's hands and rubbed it gently with his thumb. Da's skin was so thin, he had to be careful. And so yellow. Da was having trouble breathing, his body shuddered with every laboured breath. Mustn't have much time left. Daniel glanced at Caleb as he entered. Caleb's eyes glistened as he took Da's other hand, causing Daniel's eyes to fill with angry tears.

Daniel knew what death looked like. He'd seen it plenty.

How many bodies had he wheeled to the morgue as part of his job at the hospital? But he hadn't come to farewell Da. He'd come to forgive him. To talk to him. To get to know him. Not to lose him. There was little time left.

Daniel sprang from his seat. "I'm going to call Grace."

Caleb lifted his head, a surprised look on his face. Daniel didn't care if Caleb thought it useless. He had to call her. Encourage her to come. It may be her last chance.

Daniel left the bed, not taking his eyes off Da until the curtain fluttered back into position. Sprinting to the telephone box at the end of the ward, he glanced at his watch. Grace might not be up yet. Then again, she probably was. The phone rang three times before she answered.

"Daniel! What do you want at this time of the morning?"

"It's Da, Grace. He's dying. Probably only has hours left, if that." He paused, waiting for a response, but none came. "Will you come?"

Grace let out a heavy sigh. Was she considering it? *Please God, let her come.* Daniel started as Caleb opened the door of the phone box and peeked in. His heart raced. Had something happened? Drawing his eyebrows together, Daniel placed his hand over the mouthpiece as he asked the question of Caleb. When Caleb shook his head, relief flooded Daniel's body.

"Just going to get Caitlin."

Daniel smiled weakly and then turned his attention back to Grace.

"No, Daniel, I won't come." Grace's answer was measured and controlled. *How can she not come?* He didn't understand. Daniel's shoulders slumped.

"Grace, please. You'll regret it if you don't." He didn't want to plead. He wanted her to come of her own will, but he had no choice.

"Daniel, I'm not coming, and that's that. I have no wish whatsoever to see that man." Her voice had grown even more determined.

Daniel sighed dejectedly. He had to leave it. It was no use. She wasn't coming.

"Okay then. But I pray you'll change your mind."

"I won't."

~

GRACE HUNG up the receiver and fell back on her pillows. It was time to get up, but she needed a few minutes to steady the thoughts swilling in her head. *Maybe I should've agreed to see Da. Could Daniel be right? Will I regret it if I don't? Once he's dead, it'll be too late.* Her head hurt. *No, I can't. There's no good reason to see that man, dead or alive. He destroyed our family and caused Mam's death. Mam could still be alive if it hadn't been for him.*

And Brianna and I wouldn't have been sent to Aunt Hilda's...

Grace squeezed her eyes shut and buried her face in a pillow. Her heart thundered in her ears. *I'd rather kill the man myself than watch him die peacefully.* No, she would not see Thomas O'Connor. And she wouldn't regret it.

That decided, Grace slid out of bed and stepped into the shower, turning the heat up until her skin reddened like a cooked lobster. She'd push all thoughts of Da out of her mind and focus on the day ahead.

~

LIZZY'S HEART WAS HEAVY. Although Tara and Dillon were both awake and demanding her attention, her thoughts were totally focussed on Daniel and his Da. She pleaded with God to give Daniel time to say what he needed. She prayed for Daniel's emotional well-being, and that he wouldn't blame God for taking his Da away from him right now. That he'd see the bigger picture, and be happy his Da was going to a better place where there'd be no more pain or suffering. Above all, Lizzy prayed for peace for Daniel, his Da, and the rest of the family. And that those who didn't know Him, like Grace, might catch a glimpse of heaven because of the way God had blessed and changed Thomas O'Connor in the last year of his life on earth.

She couldn't physically go to the hospital with two small children, but in every other way, she was there. She needed to be strong for him, to support him in every way possible. She closed her eyes and inhaled deeply. *God, please help me be the wife Daniel needs right now.*

DANIEL TOOK a moment after hanging up the phone and leaned his head on the wall of the telephone box. Grace needed to come. The other girls had little memory of Da, and besides, he himself didn't really know them. Grace was his main concern. Always had been. *'God, I don't know what it'll take, but I plead with You to work in Grace's heart. Soften it, Lord God, and let her come. And Lord, please let me have just a minute with Da. That's all I need, and all I ask for. I'm sorry for reacting so badly before. He's a child of God, and regardless of what his life was like before, You've*

forgiven him, and so must I. Please help me see him with Your eyes. Thank you Lord God. Amen.'

Daniel pushed the door open and let it swing behind him as he headed straight back to Da. His heart was still heavy, but he had to leave Grace to God. That's what Paul had told him to do. But it was hard. He felt like screaming, or punching someone, but that wouldn't do any good.

As he passed the nurses' desk, the nurse they'd spoken to earlier stopped him.

"The doctor will be here in about half an hour and can speak with you then." Her voice was warm and caring. Daniel managed a half smile and thanked her.

He hesitated outside the curtains. All was quiet. Caleb hadn't returned. It was just him and Da. Daniel steeled himself. It was now or never. He prayed Da would have just one lucid moment. That's all he needed.

Slowly pulling the curtains apart, Daniel peeked in before sliding into the narrow area beside the bed. Taking a seat, he picked up Da's hand.

"Da, it's me, Daniel." Da didn't move. His breathing remained laboured and irregular. The tubes pumping what Daniel assumed to be pain killers into him looked stronger than the arm they were attached to. A lump rose in Daniel's throat. He'd just have to talk, and trust Da would hear the words. He might not get another opportunity.

Daniel gulped and tried to push the lump in his throat away.

"Da, I'm sorry I ran out yesterday. Silly of me." Daniel fought back his tears. "When I saw you there, and heard you speak about 'seeing the light', and being sorry for what you did to us and Mam, I couldn't cope, and I ran. I'm sorry. I should've stayed. Now I might not even get the chance to speak with you, other than like this."

Daniel paused and took a deep breath, pushing back the tears stinging his eyes.

"Da, open your eyes, please, just once, so I can see you properly. If you can hear me, can you try?" Daniel waited. While he waited, he prayed. His pulse quickened. *Did Da's eyes just flutter?*

"Da, please try again." Daniel squeezed Da's hand tighter and leaned closer to his face. No, he hadn't imagined it. Da's eyes flickered and his hand twitched. Tears welled in Daniel's eyes.

"Da, it's Daniel. Can you hear me?"

Da's eyes flickered open and then closed. Daniel held his breath.

"This is so hard, Da. I didn't want to see you, you know that? But I'm glad I did. Glad I heard you speak yesterday, and I truly believe you're sorry for the past. I would never have believed it if I hadn't seen and heard it myself, but God's done something in me, Da, and I don't hate you anymore."

Daniel bit his lip and forced himself to continue. "Thinking of all the wasted years makes me sad, but knowing you're going to be with God and that He's forgiven you, makes the hurt easier to bear." Daniel took another deep breath as he peered into Da's face. *Come on Da, wake up.*

He pushed back his tears. "Da, I know you didn't mean to hurt us. There's something evil about drink when it takes hold of a person. I know what it's like. Been there myself. I'm just so glad I 'saw the light' now, and I'm determined to stay strong and become a good husband and father. God's blessed me with a beautiful wife, Da. Should see her." Daniel smiled and let out a small chuckle as he thought of Lizzy.

"She loves the Lord, and she's smart, and I love her so much. I've promised never to hurt her again, Da. Makes me sick in the stomach when I think how close I came to losing her. And my little boy, Da. His name's Dillon. Named after our Dillon. Remember him, Da? Only lived a few hours. Broke Mam's heart when he died."

Daniel paused and closed his eyes for a moment. It'd been so hard when Da left, not long after Dillon died. Sure, they all felt safer. There were no more beatings, but despite that, they all expected to see him walk in the door every night. But he never did. Strange, really, because although they hated him and were scared of him, he was still their Da, and the place felt empty without him.

Daniel sighed heavily as he gave Da's hand a light squeeze. "But that's all in the past now, Da. Wish we had more time together, but this is all we've got." Daniel's voice faltered. He had to say it. He swallowed hard and took a deep breath.

"Da, I just want to say that I forgive you, and I love you." His eyes blurred with tears, but when Da squeezed his hand, Daniel couldn't stop them falling. Da had heard him.

No more words were needed. He'd connected with Da, and peace floated through his body.

"Can I pray, Da?" Would Da respond, or had his mind shut down? A small flicker in his eyes. Daniel smiled and squeezed Da's hand gently.

"Lord God, our loving Heavenly Father, we come to You today as men who've known both sides of the track, but are so glad we're on Your side now, Lord God. Thank You for loving us so much, and for forgiving us when we didn't deserve it. Thank You for opening our eyes to the truth of the gospel, and for placing your love and peace deep inside us. Thank You for giving me the chance to see Da before he goes to be with You." Daniel wiped his eyes. "Lord God, You know my heart's breaking, but I know You'll be my comfort in the days ahead. And Lord God, I just pray one more thing. Will You soften Grace's heart? Please, Lord God? Bless Da. Fill him with Your peace, and comfort him. In Jesus' precious name, Amen."

Daniel lifted his head and squeezed Da's hand. As he did, a stronger hand settled on his own shoulder. Caleb stood behind him, tears rolling down his cheeks. Caitlin's arm was around Caleb's waist and she leaned on his shoulder, tears also streaming down her cheeks.

Da's body shuddered, and he took his last breath.

Daniel expected he'd be distraught, but instead, warm calm flowed through his body. The pain on Da's face only moments earlier had now been replaced with serenity. God had answered his prayer.

Daniel leaned down and placed a gentle kiss on Da's hollow cheek.

"God bless you, Da."

He stood and swapped places with Caleb. Caitlin drew him close and hugged him. Wrapped in her arms, Daniel allowed himself to weep.

CHAPTER 11

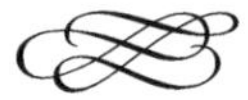

When the doctor finally arrived just after Da died, he'd said Da had been offered a new liver a week before but had refused it. No-one knew. Daniel expected to be annoyed and angry, but instead felt saddened. Da must have been desperate to go home. He could have had a number of years left with his family. But his life had been rough, and Daniel guessed he was tired of living. Daniel prayed he was enjoying his new body, and sent a glance heavenward, letting out a small chuckle.

Da's funeral was held three days later.

"What are you laughing at, Daniel?" Lizzy grabbed his arm and peered into his eyes, a quizzical look on her face.

"Oh, just thinking of Da up there, looking down on us all. He's probably having a good old chuckle too." He grabbed her hand. "Come on, let's go."

They headed into the small chapel. Only immediate family and a few friends were expected to attend. Da had lost touch with all his old drinking buddies, and Michael O'Leary from next door had passed on several years earlier. But the chapel was full. Daniel was shocked. Who were all these people? He led Lizzy to the front seat where Caleb and Caitlin were already seated.

Daniel leaned closer to Caleb. "Who are all the people?"

Caleb's eyes twinkled. "All Da's friends from the centre. Patients and workers. Left his mark on them all, so it seems."

Daniel shook his head and chuckled once again. If only he'd had the chance to get to know Da sooner. But would he have made the trip earlier? *Probably not.*

Daniel leaned closer again and raised his eyebrows. "Grace?"

Caleb shook his head, his shoulders drooping. Aislin and Alana and their partners sat to the right, and Daniel nodded and smiled when he caught their eyes. Should get to know them. They were his sisters too, after all. Beside them, another man sat. Muscle upon muscle bulged in his folded arms, almost splitting his tight fitting shirt. A spark of recognition flickered in Daniel's mind. *Brendan?* Caleb nodded. "They let him out for the funeral."

Daniel turned and faced the front, inhaling slowly. *If only Grace was here.*

~

GRACE PAUSED OUTSIDE THE CHAPEL. She pulled her cigarette case out of her bag and lit up. She didn't smoke often, but she needed one now. Her hands shook as she took a deep drag. It's not too late to get out of here. No-one had seen her. Lizzy's words at dinner last night played over in her mind; *'You'll only get one chance, Grace. Think about it?' One chance...* She'd missed the chance to see Da alive. Could she miss the chance to farewell him in death and live with the guilt for the rest of her life? Even if she held no love for Da whatsoever? *No, I need to be here.*

She took a few quick drags and then ground the cigarette out with the toe of her stiletto, straightened her snugly fitting mid length black dress, and tip-toed into the tiny chapel, taking a seat at the very back just as the minister stood to begin the service. She sat low in the seat to avoid being seen.

The number of mourners was surprising. Were these all Da's friends? Surely not. They all looked normal, not the drunkards she remembered him cohorting with. The minister, wearing the Salvation Army uniform, had a warm and engaging manner. He welcomed everyone, and then prayed. How long had it been since Grace had bowed her head in prayer? Mam used to make them pray every night at the dinner table. As did Aunt Hilda. But Grace had only bowed her head then because she had to. The day Mam's body had been lowered into the ground was the day Grace told God she'd never talk to him ever again. And she hadn't.

Hearing the minister talk about Da was like hearing him talk about someone else. She didn't know the person he referred to. Kind, funny, caring? *Not the Da she knew.* And the stream of people who got up and spoke lovingly about him, saying they'd miss his kind words and encouraging ways. An inspiration. *What? Da? An inspiration? Am I even at the right funeral?*

Caleb stood and faced the gathering. His hands shook, and he blinked rapidly. He cleared his throat and seemed to settle.

"Thank you all for coming today to farewell Thomas Rory O'Connor, Da." His gaze for a moment settled on Daniel, Aislin, Alana and no, don't tell me, is that Brendan? *How did he get out?*

Grace wriggled uncomfortably in her seat.

Caleb returned his attention to the mourners. "Thomas, *Da*, found the Lord just under a year ago, thanks to some of you here who didn't give up on him." Caleb paused and inhaled deeply, his eyes blinking rapidly. He took another deep breath. "For your commitment and dedication to our Da's spiritual and physical welfare, my family and I are truly grateful." Caleb looked around, his eyes soft but steady.

"Da wasn't an easy man to live with in his younger years, as most of you know. He didn't hold back in telling people what a terrible father and husband he'd been, and how he regretted not 'seeing the light' earlier. He's an amazing testimony to the power of God to change people, regardless of their pasts, making them clean and new on the inside. A pity his body let him down in the end, but he accepted that the choices he made as a young man resulted in that, and was prepared to accept the consequences. He knew where he was going, and Da," Caleb glanced upwards, "I know you're probably up there looking down on us and having a good ol' chuckle, but we're going to miss you. We're proud of the man you became, and we just want to say we love you."

Caleb's voice caught, and tears streamed down his face. Daniel rose and stood beside him, placing his hand on Caleb's shoulder.

Grace fought back tears of her own and had trouble breathing. This wasn't expected. She swallowed hard, pushing the lump in her throat away. Her stomach churned. *Should have seen Da when he was alive. Now I'll never have the chance.* She pulled a tissue out of her bag and wiped her eyes. *This is stupid. I hate the man.*

Despite hearing all the testimonies of what Da had been like in the last year of his life, Grace still couldn't accept he'd changed that much. It just wasn't possible. Someone who'd been as despicable as he'd been didn't change overnight. They didn't know what they were talking about. She grabbed her bag and started to stand, but something held her back. The organist began playing a hymn, and the melody tugged at Grace's heart. She'd heard it before. Mam used to hum it as she sat by the kids' beds waiting for them to fall asleep.

'The Lord's my shepherd, I'll not want;

He makes me down to lie

In pastures green; He leadeth me

The quiet waters by.'

Grace stood and listened. She tried to join in, but the words caught in her throat. *The emotion of the moment. Nothing else to it.* But as much as she wanted to leave, her feet wouldn't budge.

~

DANIEL LIFTED his end of the coffin and placed it carefully on his left shoulder. He steeled himself. This wasn't going to be easy. The burden on his shoulder was nothing compared to the burden in his heart.

The organ began playing 'Blessed Assurance' as the three

brothers and the minister carried Da slowly towards the hearse waiting outside.

Daniel caught Lizzy's eye, and a hard lump formed in his throat. He swallowed, forcing it down. He stared ahead, but a figure standing at the back caught his eye ... *Grace? Can't be...* His pulse quickened. Had she come after all? He looked more closely. *Yes, it's Grace.* Daniel's heart soared. *Thank you, thank you, God.* Grace lowered her eyes, but not quickly enough. He held her gaze for just a moment. She'd been crying.

Daniel hoped Lizzy would notice Grace. There was nothing he could do, but he prayed Grace would stay.

The short walk to the door through the group of mourners and out to the hearse was the hardest walk Daniel had ever made. Despite the sorrow of the moment, he knew Da wasn't in the coffin. Sure, his body lay there, but his spirit was elsewhere. Da lived on, but with a new body, in a new home. As the coffin was lowered into the hearse, God's peace settled in Daniel's heart. Da was safe and secure in the Saviour's arms, of that he was sure. *Thank you, blessed God.*

With the coffin in place, Daniel turned and searched the crowd for Grace. His heart lifted as he saw her standing with Lizzy. Leaving Caleb and Brendan, he made his way through the gathering towards Grace and Lizzy. He couldn't believe Grace had actually come. An answer to prayer. *Another one.*

"Grace, so glad you came." Daniel placed a kiss on her cheek and hugged her tightly. Grace clung to him. God was doing a work in her life, of that he was sure.

She finally pulled away. Lizzy offered her a tissue and Grace wiped her face and blew her nose. Her mascara had run a little and her eyes were puffy and red.

"I'm sorry," she said, dabbing her eyes.

Daniel squeezed her hand. "It doesn't matter. Are you okay?"

Grace blew her nose.

"Think so." She breathed deeply and straightened herself. In her stilettos, she stood eye to eye with Daniel.

"I didn't think you'd come."

"Hadn't planned on it." She rolled her eyes. "Conscience got to me."

"Glad it did, Grace. Glad it did." Daniel smiled at her warmly. "Will you come to the burial? Be special if you did."

"Don't know. Give me a minute to think."

"No problem, Grace. There's no hurry."

Grace gave him a weak smile, and then turned to Caitlin and Caleb who'd just joined them.

Daniel took Lizzy's hand and stood to the side. He needed a moment to gather himself. Grace turning up had thrown him. But he was so glad she'd come. God really was doing something in her life. But he had to tread carefully. No pushing. If she didn't want to come to the burial, he'd have to let it be. *But God, please let her...*

"You okay, Daniel?" Lizzy peered up at him, concern filling her eyes.

"Yes, my love. A little overwhelmed, that's all." Slipping his arm around her waist, he pulled her close and thanked God once again for bringing Lizzy into his life. She'd become his soul mate. His best friend, and he couldn't live without her. Strange how a funeral brings clarity to everything. Makes you evaluate your own life choices, and as a result, makes you appreciate those most important to you.

Daniel leaned back and studied her. How he loved this woman God had brought into his life. He loved the way she supported and encouraged him and never gave up on him. Sometimes she got a little impatient, but he loved that she cared enough to want the best for him. His heart overflowed with love for her.

"What are you thinking, Daniel?" Lizzy tilted her head slightly, a bemused look on her face.

Daniel chuckled. He'd been caught out, but he didn't care. He lifted her chin with the tip of his finger.

"Lizzy, I don't say this often enough, but I love you."

A small smile came to Lizzy's face and her eyes glistened. "And I love you too, Daniel O'Connor. And I couldn't be prouder of you than I am at this minute."

Leaning forward, Lizzy kissed him gently. He returned her kiss and draped his arm around her shoulder before rejoining the others.

THE GROUP HAD GROWN in size, with Aislin, Alana and their partners joining Caleb, Caitlin and Grace, as well as Brendan and aunts and uncles Daniel hadn't seen for a long time. Daniel stood and listened. These were his family, his roots, but as much as he now realised he loved them, his future rested with the woman beside him. Something stirred deep inside him. He didn't know what they were, but he was impatient to find out what plans God had for their lives. But right now, Da had to be buried.

Daniel moved closer to Grace and gently placed his hand on her shoulder.

"Coming?"

Grace lifted her eyes and nodded.

"I'm glad." Daniel's chest expanded and he smiled broadly.

THE SMALL PROCESSION of cars followed the hearse to Da's final resting place. The family had debated whether Da should be buried next to Mam or not. In the end they'd agreed he should. "Mam never stopped praying for him," Caleb had said. "She loved him, despite all he did to her. I think she'd want him laid to rest beside her."

Not that it really mattered. It was only his body, but to the family left behind, at least they could now remember both parents together.

The grave had been dug the day before, and the rich earthy smell lingered in the air. As Daniel and the other men lowered Da's coffin slowly into the ground, the group began to sing 'Amazing Grace'. Daniel's heart was heavy, but as he joined hands with Lizzy and Grace, the heaviness was replaced with God's peace.

He closed his eyes as the minister gave the final blessing, and squeezing Grace's hand, prayed God would touch her heart.

"In sure and certain hope of the resurrection to eternal life through our Lord Jesus Christ, we commend to Almighty God our brother Thomas, and we commiT this body to the ground; earth to earth, ashes to ashes, dust to dust. The Lord bless him and keep him, the Lord make his face to shine upon him and be gracious unto him, the Lord lift up His countenance upon him and give him peace. Amen."

Caleb threw the first shovel of earth onto Da's coffin, the thud echoing in Daniel's heart. Daniel followed. Grace bent down and picked up a handful of earth, and threw it onto the coffin. Tears streamed down her face. Daniel wrapped his arms around Grace and comforted her.

"He's gone to be with the Lord," Daniel whispered as he stroked her hair. *Lord, please let this be a defining moment for Grace.*

The group held hands and sang another hymn before the minister said the closing prayer. It was over. It felt strange. Da was buried. His body was gone, and he would now live on in memory only. Daniel was so glad he'd had the opportunity to speak with Da before he died, and to witness the new life God had breathed into his soul. God may not have healed his body, but he'd done better than that. He'd given him new life. Life that would go on for eternity. No-one could want more than that.

Lizzy slipped her arm around Daniel's waist, and he pulled her close. The two most precious women in his life, wrapped tightly in his arms. What a blessed man he was.

The sound of cars starting up interrupted the moment. Life would go on.

As he walked slowly back towards the waiting cars, Daniel turned his head and looked to his right. Somewhere over there, Ciara and baby Rachel were buried. Another life, another story. Sorrow for all that had happened tugged at his heart, but God had forgiven him and allowed him to move on. He should have supported Ciara in her grief, not deserted her. *What a despicable person I was.* But he'd been young and ignorant. He didn't know how to cope with his own grief, let alone help her.

He could allow the sorrow he felt now over what happened to overwhelm him. But it truly was in the past, and nothing he could do now would change it.

"Do you want to go there?" Lizzy asked quietly.

How does she know? She never ceases to amaze me. Daniel took a deep slow breath.

"No, I don't. They're my past, Lizzy. I want to move on. With you." He squeezed her hand and gave her a look that contained all the love God had poured into his heart for her.

SEVERAL DAYS LATER, as Daniel and Lizzy stood leaning on the railings at the stern of the ship heading back to Liverpool, Daniel was deep in thought. He'd become a lot more introspective of late. Maybe it was God's way of talking to him, because he often had thoughts floating through his mind that could only have come from God. But right now, his thoughts were on Lizzy and their future together. He was sure God had something special planned for them, but didn't know what. But he needed to know one thing.

"Lizzy, do you ever regret not having a proper wedding?"

Lizzy spun around, startled.

"What made you ask that?"

"Not sure, really. I was just thinking about all we've been through." He pulled her to him and wrapped his arms around her waist, gazing into her curious eyes. "The way we got married without your parents knowing, the way I treated you so badly, and how thankful I was when you came back and led me to the Lord." He lifted a hand to her face and gently brushed back a lock of hair. "Don't most girls dream of a big wedding? I know you turned your father's offer down, but I sometimes wonder if you're sad about missing out on all that." Daniel tilted his head slightly, his eyes full of love and concern. "Are you?"

Lizzy grinned, letting out a small laugh. "I guess you're right. Most girls do dream of a fairy tale wedding, but you know, it really is just one day. To be honest, I guess sometimes I do feel a little sad, but it's not the fairy tale wedding with all the trimmings that makes a marriage work. It's what comes after that's more important."

"Would you like to have one, anyway? I can sort something if you do."

Lizzy laughed and hit him playfully. "Don't be silly, Daniel. It's too late for all that, and I really don't care that much." Turning serious, Lizzy continued. "But I would like to renew our vows before God one day soon."

"That's a grand idea, Lizzy." Daniel flashed a brilliant smile. "Let's do it now!"

"Now! What do you mean?"

"Like right here, right now. God's here with us. We don't need anyone else to be present. Just you, me, God," Daniel looked down, "and baby Dillon."

Lizzy's eyes twinkled and her grin broadened into a full blown smile. "Okay, let's do it."

Daniel took both of Lizzy's hands and squeezed them, his eyes settling on hers. He took a deep breath.

"Elizabeth, *Lizzy*, before God our Father, who brought us together and gave us the gift of love, I promise to be faithful to you and to love and cherish you as long as we both shall live. Because of you, I laugh, I smile, I dare to dream again. I look forward with great joy to spending the rest of my life with you, caring for you, nurturing you, and being there for you in all God has in store for us."

Daniel leaned forward and kissed Lizzy gently on the lips.

Lizzy wiped her tears and took Daniel's hands in hers. "Have you been practicing that?" She let out a small laugh.

"Maybe..." He grinned at her mischievously.

Lizzy straightened herself and inhaled slowly. "Okay, it's my turn."

"Daniel O'Connor, with God as my witness, I promise to love and cherish you forever. I look forward to dancing with you in times of joy, to lifting you up in times of sadness, to rejoicing with you in times of good health, and to caring for you in times of illness. I promise to turn to you for comfort, for encouragement, and for inspiration. I love you and I know that this love is from God. I'll thank Him every day for bringing you into my life."

Lizzy squeezed Daniel's hands and held his unwavering gaze before kissing him.

Daniel leaned down and lifted Dillon out of his push chair. Lizzy placed her hand on Dillon's head as Daniel cradled him in his arms.

"And Lord God, we thank You for entrusting Dillon, this precious little boy, into our care. Together, Lizzy and I promise to make our home a place where he'll feel safe and loved, and where he'll grow up learning Your ways. Give us wisdom to raise Dillon the way You would have us, to be an example to him of godly love. Let him grow to love You, and may he discover the joy of Your presence in his life. We dedicate him to You now, Lord God. Bless his wee little life, we pray. Amen."

Daniel kissed Dillon's little head and then looked up at Lizzy. His heart overflowed with love for her. What a blessed man he was.

"Lizzy, I don't know what the Lord's got planned for us, but I know He's got something special in mind. I feel it deep within me. There's a real stirring of my spirit." He squeezed her hand and took a deep breath. "I'm so thankful He gave me another chance, and I want to live my life for Him. With you."

"Daniel, that's exactly what I feel. God will show us in His time. We just have to be patient."

Daniel laughed. "Good one, Liz! Coming from you, that's a hoot!"

Lizzy slapped him playfully. Laughing, he pulled her close and lowered his mouth over hers, but had to ply baby Dillon's fingers from between their lips before he could kiss her thoroughly.

~

SECRETS AND SACRIFICE - BONUS CHAPTER

"THE SHADOWS SERIES BOOK 4"

CHAPTER 1

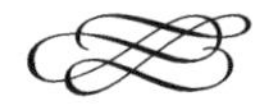

Belfast 1985

GRACE ROSE, pausing momentarily before marching to the front of the court room. The twelve members of the jury sat in their box, looking weary after a week of listening to the despicable deeds of Donal Patrick O'Malley. Now it was up to her to convince them they should find him guilty of murder.

A hush fell over the court room as Grace cast her gaze over them. She'd prepared for this moment, but would it be enough? Niall would no doubt have a brilliant closing argument. Hers had to dazzle.

Grace took a deep breath to steady herself, but just as she opened her mouth to speak, a tall, thin man with darkish hair, shaved on the sides and spiked on top, entered the room, catching her attention. Grace's body stiffened. *Caleb? No, it can't be. Or could it?* Her brother never came to court, even when she was prosecuting a high profile case such as this. But it sure looked like him. Grace's heart raced and a feeling of dread flooded her body. He would only come if something bad had happened. Regardless, she'd have to ignore him and focus on the job at hand. Besides, it might not even be him.

Returning her attention to the jury, she began her closing arguments, affording herself the occasional glance at the man. It was Caleb, no doubt about it. His face, normally pale, was deathly white. Something bad must have happened.

Somehow she focused on her speech. She needed to win. No way could she allow O'Malley to walk free after beating his wife to death, but with Caleb sitting in the back, it was a challenge. Finally, she reached her conclusion. "So, members of the jury, after all you've heard, I beg you to find the accused, Donal Patrick O'Malley, guilty as charged. Thank you."

Grace's stomach tightened as her gaze met Caleb's on her short walk back to her seat. She was tempted to go to him, but that would be breaking protocol. She'd have to wait to find out what had happened.

Her head hurt. She'd put everything she had into her speech, and now she felt drained. Normally she could relax a little after her job was done, but now... with Caleb sitting behind her? Impossible.

Bryan leaned over and offered his congratulations. Grace gave him a half smile. Bryan, her trusted assistant and most ardent advocate, would always say she'd done well, even if she hadn't.

Grace inhaled deeply to settle herself as the Judge called for the Defendant's closing arguments. Niall stood, and as he walked to the front of the room, she chastised herself for allowing him to unnerve her. Even after a week of seeing him every day, she failed to treat him like any other man. *Because he wasn't any other man.*

He'd aged a little. Small flecks of grey peppered the dark hair poking out from under his wig, only serving to increase his appeal. He'd also changed. It wasn't just the suit. Or his lean body. There was something else. Grace had seen it from the front of the court room when he'd caught her eye on the first day of the trial. A sadness, and no doubt, she was partly responsible. But it puzzled her—surely three years in London would have given him enough time for him to move on.

He wasn't quite the same man she'd fallen in love with in the heady days of college, but his nearness still stirred something deep inside her.

A tap on her shoulder jolted her, and she looked up into a clerk's concerned eyes.

"Miss, your brother's asking to see you urgently."

Grace spun around. *It must be bad.*

Her stomach churned as she grasped the rail and pulled herself up before making her way as unobtrusively as possible to the back of the room.

Sliding into the seat, Grace grabbed Caleb's thin arm and leaned close to him. She looked into his troubled eyes. "What's happened, Caleb?"

"Come outside, Grace." Caleb took her arm and led her into the foyer as Niall began his closing argument. She shouldn't leave, but this sounded like an emergency, and besides, Bryan was more than capable of taking notes.

"What's wrong, Caleb? It's not Caitlin, is it? Or the girls?" Grace gripped him tighter. "Please don't tell me it's the girls."

Caleb faced her. "If you stop talking, I'll tell you."

Grace pulled herself up. He was right... she needed to stop talking. She was jumping to conclusions. Best get the facts.

"Okay. Who?" Grace's heart beat faster. Was she ready to find out?

Caleb gulped, his protruding Adam's apple bobbing in his heavily tattooed neck.

"Brianna's been found."

Grace's eyes widened and she grabbed his arm again.

"Brianna? Where is she? Is she okay?"

Caleb paused, holding Grace's gaze.

"She can't be..."

"She's alive, Grace, but only just. She was found this morning, unconscious."

Grace covered her mouth with her hand. "I thought you were going to say she was dead..." She let out a huge sigh. Was it wrong to be relieved when your sister had been found unconscious?

"Where was she?"

"In a dingy apartment. Looks like an overdose."

"She promised." Grace huffed and narrowed her eyes. "She promised, Caleb. If only she'd kept her word."

"It's not that simple, Grace. You know that."

Grace sighed heavily. "Yes, I do. Where is she?"

"St. Vincent's. I'm going now. Can you come?"

"Not yet. But I will as soon as I can. Have you called the others?"

Caleb ran his hand along the side of his shaved head. "No—

I only just found out and I came straight here. I'll call them now."

Grace pulled a cigarette from under her robe and lit up. She didn't offer one to Caleb. "She'd better pull through." She took several quick puffs.

"Yes, she'd better. Caitlin's at home praying. She said that's the best thing she can do to help."

Grace rolled her eyes. *That's exactly what Caleb's wife, Caitlin, would do.*

Caleb leaned in and hugged Grace. "Come as soon as you can."

Grace hugged him back and held his gaze. "You're a good brother, Caleb."

As she watched Caleb hurry off, she took several more quick drags on her cigarette before grinding it out in an ashtray on the windowsill.

When she re-entered the court room, Niall was towards the end of his speech. Grace remained at the back to avoid creating a disturbance. It was difficult to focus. All she could think of was Brianna, her younger sister, lying in hospital, unconscious. *What if she dies?* Grace needed to get there as quickly as possible. But what could she do to help? At least Caitlin could pray. Grace couldn't even do that. It didn't matter. Being there would be enough.

GRACE ALLOWED her gaze to follow Niall as he took his seat. Just the look of him stirred her insides. *Why did he come back to Belfast? Surely London would have been more exciting.*

Moving forward quietly, she slid into her seat beside Bryan as a general buzz filled the room.

Bryan lifted his head and looked at her.

"Miss, are you alright?" Bryan's concern for her always warmed her heart.

"Yes, Bryan. Thank you. Just some family issues. I'll be okay." She gave him a weak smile.

Judge Atkinson cleared his throat, and the buzz in the court room died down.

"Thank you, members of the jury. We'll adjourn for now and reconvene at nine o'clock tomorrow for final instructions. Good night, and thank you for your time."

Everyone rose as the Judge stood and exited the room. Gathering her papers, Grace tossed them into her brief case.

"I've got to go, Bryan. But how did he do?" She nodded her head towards Niall who stood with his team on the opposite side of the bench. An unwelcome pang of jealousy stabbed her as a young attractive blond hung on his every word.

"Oh, he did well, as expected, but I think we've got it."

"Nothing's ever definite until the jury comes back. You know that, Bryan."

"Yes, Miss, I do. They can go either way. But if I were a betting man, I'd bet on you."

"Oh Bryan. What would I do without you?" Grace let out a small laugh. "I really do have to fly. I'll see you in the morning."

"Okay, Miss. Good night."

"Good night, Bryan." Grace swept her robe around her shoulders and hurried towards the exit, shooting one quick look at Niall before leaving the room. The blond was standing way too close. Grace sighed dejectedly. *Will I ever get over him?*

Stupid, really. It was her fault they'd broken up. She didn't want to get married. He did. *Too late now.* The blond had her hooks into him.

Grace glanced at her watch. She should change, but no, time was of the essence—she'd go straight to the hospital. What if something happened to Brianna in the time it took to return to Chambers?

AS GRACE TURNED into Frew Lane, a biting wind caught her robe and sent it flying. Grabbing it, she pulled it tighter, but as she paused, a deep voice she'd know anywhere called out.

Grace stopped and turned. Niall was jogging towards her. Her heart fluttered. *Drat the man! How does he do that?*

Niall stopped and stood before her, wig in hand, his chest expanding and contracting heavily as he caught his breath.

"Grace, what's happened? I saw you disappear." His warm brown eyes gazed into hers as he touched her arm lightly, threatening to dismantle her resolve to remain aloof. "You don't look too good..."

Grace lowered her eyes. Allowing him back into her life would be asking for trouble. But she could surely do with a friend right now. No. She was strong, and she didn't need anyone. *Especially Niall. Get a grip, Grace.*

She inhaled deeply and lifted her head. "It's nothing, really, Niall. Just a small family matter."

Niall tilted his head, a quizzical look on his way too handsome face. "Doesn't look like that to me, Grace." He knew her too well. "Where are you racing off to?"

Grace shook her head and pulled her robe higher around

her neck. A light drizzle had begun to fall. People scurried past, hurrying to get home before the skies opened up. Niall opened the umbrella he'd been holding in one hand and held it over her. The gentleman as always.

"Come on, Grace, let's get out of this. Let me drive you to wherever you're going."

Grace stiffened. Should she let her defences down just a little? If she did, would she be able to put them back up again? Or would she succumb to Niall's charms and let all her resolves fly out the window? She looked into the eyes of the only man she'd ever loved and weakened.

Niall's hand rested on her elbow as he guided her towards the car park around the corner, stopping in front of a silver, 1982 Alfa Romeo Spider. Grace cast her eyes over the tiny sports car and approved. She and Niall had always shared a penchant for fast cars.

Niall's seatbelt clicked. As he turned the key, the Spider sprang to life, the roar of the engine thrilling her. He turned and looked at her. "So, where are we off to?"

Grace had to tear her eyes from his before she did something she'd regret. He was way too close for comfort.

"St. Vincent's." Grace's gaze was firmly fixed on the road ahead. "Brianna's overdosed."

~

To continue Grace's story, get your copy here:

http://julietteduncan.com/secrets-sacrifice/

NOTE FROM THE AUTHOR

I truly hope you've enjoyed Lizzy and Daniel's story, and that you've been touched by their unfolding relationship with each other and with God. Make sure you follow their continuing story in ***"Secrets and Sacrifice"***, available now on Amazon. To get notified of my new releases, why not join my mailing list?

Visit www.julietteduncan.com/subscribe to join, and as a thank you for signing up, you'll also receive a **free short story.**

Finally, could I ask you a favor? Would you help other people find this box set by writing a review and telling them why you liked it? Honest reviews of my books help bring them to the attention of other readers just like yourself, and I'd be very grateful if you could spare just five minutes to leave a review (it can be as short as you like).

In gratitude,

Juliette

ALSO BY JULIETTE DUNCAN

Secrets and Sacrifice

***BOOK 4 of "The Shadows Series"**, can also be read as a stand-alone novel.*

When Grace O'Connor arrives in the Scottish Highlands, she's hiding a secret and trailing more baggage than she cares to admit. Grace's sister, Brianna, has a history linked to Grace's secret. There, amongst the rugged Scottish Highlands and a community of caring, loving Christians, Grace meets the handsome Ryan MacGregor, an ex-military Paratrooper with a history of his own. As the secrets of Grace's past unravel and the sacrifices she's made are thrown back at her, Grace faces the biggest decision of her life. As everything Grace has believed is turned upside down, she realizes that the walls she's worked so hard at building have been for no reason whatsoever, and she now needs to discover who she really is.

Praise for "Secrets and Sacrifice"

"I think this may be my favorite book by Juliette so far. There is an element of suspense that is woven into the whole book. The characters are very well developed and the book keeps your interest throughout. It can be read as a stand-alone book, but if you have read the (Shadows) series, you will recognize the characters and have a deeper understanding. I highly recommend this book for anyone that enjoys a good Christian romance." Mary

"Every time Juliette Duncan releases another book I can't wait to read it. Her latest book about Grace did not disappoint and I read it every spare moment I got. Grace's secret was not what I expected and the story had interesting turns that kept me captivated. I love the way that Juliette brings the word of God into her stories. This is another book you must read but once you start don't be surprised if you can't put it down!" Ann

The True Love Series

After her long-term relationship falls apart, Tessa Scott is left questioning God's plan for her life, and she's feeling vulnerable and unsure of how to move forward.

Ben Williams is struggling to keep the pieces of his life together after his wife of fourteen years walks out on him and their teenage son. Tessa's housemate inadvertently sets up a meeting between the two of them, triggering a chain of events neither expected. Be prepared for a roller-coaster ride of emotions as Tessa, Ben and Jayden do life together and learn to trust God to meet their every need.

Praise for "The True Love Series"

"These books are so good you won't be able to stop reading them. The characters in the books are very special people who will feel like they are part of your family." Debbie J

The Precious Love Series Book 1 - Forever Cherished

"Forever Cherished" is a stand-alone novel, but follows on from "The True Love Series" books. Now Tessa is living in the country, she wants to share her and Ben's blessings with others, but when a sad, lonely woman comes to stay, Tessa starts to think she's bitten off more than she can chew, and has to rely on her faith at every turn. Leah Maloney is carrying a truck-load of disappointments and has almost given up on life. Her older sister arranges for her to spend time at 'Misty Morn', but Leah is suspicious of her sister's motives.

Praise for "Forever Cherished"

"Another amazing story of God's love and the amazing ways he works in our lives." Ruth H

Hank and Sarah - A Love Story, ***the Prequel to "The Madeleine Richards Series" is a FREE thank you gift for joining my mailing list. You'll also be the first to hear about my next books and get exclusive sneak previews. Get your free copy at www.julietteduncan.com/subscribe***

The Madeleine Richards Series Although the 3 book series is intended mainly for pre-teen/Middle Grade girls, it's been read and enjoyed by people of all ages.

ABOUT THE AUTHOR

Juliette Duncan is a Christian fiction author, passionate about writing stories that will touch her readers' hearts and make a difference in their lives. Although a trained school teacher, Juliette spent many years working alongside her husband in their own business, but is now relishing the opportunity to follow her passion for writing stories she herself would love to read. Based in Brisbane, Australia, Juliette and her husband have five adult children, seven grandchildren, and an elderly long haired dachshund.Apart from writing, Juliette loves exploring the great world we live in, and has travelled extensively, both within Australia and overseas. She also enjoys social dancing and eating out.

Connect with Juliette:

Email: juliette@julietteduncan.com

Website: www.julietteduncan.com

Facebook: www.facebook.com/JulietteDuncanAuthor

Twitter: https://twitter.com/Juliette_Duncan

Made in the USA
Middletown, DE
14 June 2021